Praise for

The RHINO in Right Field

★"Laugh-out-loud fun with a wonderful
cast of characters. A winner in every way."
—*KIRKUS REVIEWS*, **STARRED REVIEW**

"DeKeyser skillfully melds
historical details of 1948 Milwaukee with fast-paced
action and humor. . . . A recommended purchase
for large middle grade collections."
—*SCHOOL LIBRARY JOURNAL*

"Funny and good-hearted."
—*PUBLISHERS WEEKLY*

"[A] warm, wonderful novel."
—*SHELF AWARENESS FOR READERS*

"Accessible, detailed, and charmingly
genuine. . . . A solid home run."
—*BOOKLIST ONLINE*

ALSO BY STACY DeKEYSER

The Brixen Witch
One Witch at a Time

STACY DeKEYSER

The RHINO in Right Field

MARGARET K. McELDERRY BOOKS
NEW YORK LONDON TORONTO SYDNEY NEW DELHI

If you purchased this book without a cover, you should be aware that this book is stolen property. It was reported as "unsold and destroyed" to the publisher, and neither the author nor the publisher has received any payment for this "stripped book."

MARGARET K. McELDERRY BOOKS
An imprint of Simon & Schuster Children's Publishing Division
1230 Avenue of the Americas, New York, New York 10020
This book is a work of fiction. Any references to historical events, real people, or real places are used fictitiously. Other names, characters, places, and events are products of the author's imagination, and any resemblance to actual events or places or persons, living or dead, is entirely coincidental.
Text copyright © 2018 by Stacy DeKeyser
Cover illustrations copyright © 2018 by Bill Mayer
All rights reserved, including the right of reproduction in whole or in part in any form.
MARGARET K. McELDERRY BOOKS
is a trademark of Simon & Schuster, Inc.
For information about special discounts for bulk purchases, please contact Simon & Schuster Special Sales at 1-866-506-1949 or business@simonandschuster.com.
The Simon & Schuster Speakers Bureau can bring authors to your live event. For more information or to book an event, contact the Simon & Schuster Speakers Bureau at 1-866-248-3049 or visit our website at www.simonspeakers.com.
Book design by Debra Sfetsios-Conover and Brad Mead
The text for this book was set in Palatino LT Std.
Manufactured in the United States of America
0919 OFF
First Margaret K. McElderry Books
paperback edition May 2019
10 9 8 7 6 5 4 3 2
The Library of Congress has cataloged
the hardcover edition as follows:
Names: DeKeyser, Stacy, author.
Title: The rhino in right field / Stacy DeKeyser.
Description: First edition. | New York : Margaret K. McElderry Books, [2018] | Summary: In 1948, Nikko Spirakis, twelve, loves baseball but must get past his hard-working immigrant parents—and the rhino in the outfield—to become a batboy for the local minor league team.
Identifiers: LCCN 2017032528 (print) | LCCN 2017044306 (eBook) | ISBN 9781534406261 (hardcover) | ISBN 9781534406278 (trade pbk.) | ISBN 9781534406285 (eBook)
Subjects: | CYAC: Baseball—Fiction. | Friendship—Fiction. | Family life—Wisconsin—Fiction. | Immigrants—Fiction. | Greek Americans—Fiction. | Wisconsin—History—20th century—Fiction.
Classification: LCC PZ7.D3682 (eBook) | LCC PZ7.D3682 Rhi 2018 (print) | DDC [Fic]—dc23
LC record available at https://lccn.loc.gov/2017032528

For Dad

Σε αγαπώ

CHAPTER

EVERYTHING STARTED ON the day I had that close call with Tank.

Tank lives two blocks away, so I see him almost every day, but he usually ignores me. This is probably for the best, since Tank is a rhinoceros. A 2,580-pound *Diceros bicornis* with a seventeen-inch horn, according to the sign on his fence. That fence also happened to be our right-field fence, which is how Tank and I got to know each other on a first-name basis. It was my turn to play right field, and I'll admit it: my mind wandered. If you've ever played baseball, you know what it's like. Because no one ever hits the ball to right field.

Except, of course, when they do.

It doesn't help that I'm a terrible outfielder. To be perfectly honest, I couldn't catch a fly ball to save my life.

So there I was, caught flat-footed when Pete walloped the ball. It sailed over my head and landed with a *thunk* in a pile of hay on the wrong side of the fence. Tank's side. And there was Tank, snoozing in the shade of a billboard. (CALL KING'S MOTORS AT HOPKINS 5800. YOUR SOURCE FOR GENUINE PACKARD PARTS!)

That was our last baseball. Somebody had to get it back.

And that somebody was the right fielder.

Let me say this right now: the general public does not belong in rhinoceros pens—ever. This fact is so obvious, some genius decided that a stone wall topped with a chest-high chain-link fence would be enough of a reminder. Sure, it's enough to keep a stumpy-legged rhino *in*. But it's useless at keeping a twelve-year-old kid *out*. Because here's another obvious thing: Baseballs do not belong in rhinoceros pens either. What if Tank ate the ball? That would end the game in a hurry—or at least postpone it. The truth always comes out in the end (so to speak).

The fellas gave me their usual encouragement.

"What're ya waiting for, Nick?"

"I think he's chicken, that's what I think."

"Some right fielder you are! What, are ya scared of a little ol' rhino?"

I dropped my mitt and sized up the situation: hop the fence, grab the ball, and back to safety. Six seconds, tops.

Or never. Depending on the reflexes of the rhino.

"Yep. He's chicken, all right."

"*Bawwwwk, bawk bawk . . .*"

I took a deep breath, wound myself up, and . . .

vaulted the fence, up and over ("Atta boy, Nick!")

raced to the hay pile ("Hurry up!")

grabbed the ball (That's not the ball. What *is* that?)

There's the ball!

SNORT.

"RUN! Don't look back!"

Over the top, and OUT.

Exactly 2,580 pounds of muscle crashed into the wall behind me, leaving a Tank-shaped dent in the stone. (I might be making up that last part. But everything else is true, I swear.)

I somersaulted on the ground. My heart was pounding. My pants were torn. Something smelled really bad.

But I was holding the ball.

"You did it!" said Ace, running out from shortstop.

"Holy moly, we thought you were a goner," hollered Charlie from the pitcher's mound.

Chuck just stood there in left field with his mouth hanging open.

"Look at you, Spirakis." Here came Pete, swaggering out from home plate with the bat on his shoulder. "You might live to finish sixth grade after all. Now grab your mitt and hand over that muddy ball. That was a home run and it's four to three. Still two outs."

I stood up, brushed myself off, and flipped the ball to Pete. "Not so fast, slugger. You know the rules. Anything hit into the rhino pen is an automatic out. And by the way—that ain't mud."

$\mathcal{B}$Y NOW YOU MIGHT HAVE figured out that we play ball in the zoo. This is not as crazy as it sounds. The zoo is part of the city park. In other words: public property.

There's not a lot of room, what with Tank in right field, the buffalo pen along the first-base line, and city streets on the other two sides. We don't usually have enough players for a real game, so we made up our own version and call it Scramble (because whenever the ball's in play, that's what everybody has to do).

We played two more innings, until the five-o'clock whistles blew. First, from the brewery on State Street. Then, a half second later, from the factories under the viaduct, one after another.

"Same time tomorrow?" said Pete, and we all nodded.

"Seventh inning, and it's tied at five," I said, swiping my mitt at Ace. "Your turn in right field tomorrow."

"Yeah, yeah." Ace sounded tough, but I caught him shooting a nervous glance toward the rhino pen.

We collected our gear and headed toward home. Once we were out of the park, Ace and I broke off from the group and started south, down Forty-Fourth Street. It's one of those streets where all the houses look pretty much the same: squat, brick bungalows, each one with a tiny square of lawn and a big front porch. Elm trees lining both sides of the street, heaving up the sidewalk with their roots.

Of course, the houses aren't *exactly* the same. Right now, we were walking past a house with a BEWARE OF DOG sign out front. Somewhere inside, something very small yapped to beat the band. And there was old Mr. Goldberg, waving from his porch swing as usual.

We passed a couple more houses. Someone had their windows open, even though it was still chilly, and I could hear *Dick Tracy* playing on a radio.

At the next house, Ace twitched his nose like a rabbit. "Phew! Sauerkraut at Schmitzy's again. How can they eat that stuff? It smells even worse than you do right now!"

"Very funny."

"What's the matter with you?" he said. And then the lightbulb turned on over his head. "Are you still worked up about Tank?"

I kicked at the cracks in the sidewalk. "I thought rhinos had bad eyesight."

"Very bad eyesight. Very *good* hearing. Who knew? With those tiny ears?" Ace grabbed his own ears (which weren't so tiny) and wiggled them. Then he poked me with his mitt. "You'd do it all over again if you had to. I know you would."

I felt a smile creeping across my face. "It *was* pretty swell, wasn't it?"

"Swell?" said Ace. "It was legendary! Did you get a load of Pete's face when you tossed him that brown ball? What a thing of beauty!"

"He deserved it," I said. "If I didn't know better, I'd say Pete hit that ball into Tank's yard on purpose."

Ace's eyebrows shot up. "Nah. Ya think?"

"He batted lefty," I told him. "All of a sudden he decides he's a switch hitter? He just wanted to hit the ball over the right-field fence, so *I'd* have to go after it."

"Pete's not that good," said Ace. "Or that smart. He just got lucky."

"Maybe." We stepped around a couple of girls playing hopscotch on the sidewalk. "But I think he was *hoping* to get lucky."

We were at Ace's house now, and his nose twitched again. "Hey! I smell . . . fried burgers! How great is that? Want me to see if there's extra?"

"Nicky!" called a voice from next door. My ma. "Come wash up now."

My stomach rumbled. "Maybe next time. Thanks anyway."

Ace looked past me and waved. "Hiya, Mrs. S!" He slapped me on the back. "See ya later, *Nicky*." And he darted into his house, letting the screen door slam behind him.

"I hope you choke on that burger!" I hollered after him. I turned, and there was my mother, kneeling on the front lawn with a tin bucket next to her. "Ma? What ya doing?"

"Supper," she said. "What happens to your pants?"

"Tore 'em. Playing ball."

"Again?" She sighed. Then she showed me the bucket, half filled with dark green leaves. "They look nice, *neh*? Your father's favorite."

I glanced around, and my face burned. "Aren't there enough dandelions in the backyard?"

"Not so many," said Ma, standing up and brushing at her apron. "What? I embarrass you? Your friend Azy, he doesn't mind if I pick *radikia*." She nodded toward the house next door, and she grinned. "I pick some from their yard too."

"Gee whiz, Ma! And anyway, it's Ace, not Azy."

"That's what I said. Azy." We climbed the porch steps. "Why you want him to choke? That's not a nice thing to tell your best friend."

I remembered what I'd said to Ace. "It was nothing, Ma.

Just a joke." I pulled the screen door open, and she clattered the bucket through.

"Joke? I thought you said 'choke.'" She wrinkled her nose as she squeezed past me. "What do I smell?"

"You don't want to know, Ma."

*T*HAT'LL BE NINETY-FIVE CENTS." I punched the keys on the cash register, and the drawer slid open with a *ding*.

The customer handed over a dollar bill. "Keep the change," he said. "A little Saturday bonus." He adjusted the fedora on his head and called toward the back of the shop. "Thanks again, George. Nobody can block a hat like you."

In a halo of lamplight, a small, wiry guy with glasses and bushy eyebrows waved a shoe and then bent over his work again. My father.

The customer swept out onto the sidewalk. As the door jingled shut behind him, the odor of shoe polish collided with fresh air and bus exhaust.

"Nicky?" called my father from his workbench. "Mister

Watson's shoes, they're ready. Bring me a box, *neh*?"

"Sure thing, Pop." I grabbed an empty shoe box from behind the counter, along with a sheet of blank newsprint. "Say, Pop? You think I could take off a little early today? The fellas are playing ball."

"The fellas, they're always playing ball," answered Pop, making room on the worktable.

"It's quiet today. I even dusted the tops of the shelves, where no one can see."

"Good boy," said Pop, without looking up. "You know the rules, Nicky. Saturday, it's a working day. We are open until five o'clock."

"But, Pop—"

He held up a finger, which meant the discussion was over.

It wasn't fair. Nobody else had a Saturday job. Well, Charlie had a weekend paper route, but he was always finished by breakfast. It's not that I hated working in the shop, exactly. I got decent tips, and it was better than getting up when it was still dark and trudging around with a sack of newspapers slung over your shoulder. But who wants to be cooped up when it's Saturday afternoon and the sun is shining and the grass is smelling sweet?

Pop inspected the pair of oxfords he'd been working on. They weren't new shoes, but no one needed to bring new shoes to the Elegant Shoe Repair and Hat Shop. This pair had new soles and new laces, and they'd been buffed to a soft sheen. "I tell you what," Pop said, lining the shoe box with the newsprint. "If nobody comes in before three o'clock, you can go. Just this once."

The clock on the wall read two forty-five. It was a snowball's chance, but it was a chance.

Pop nestled the shoes into the box as carefully as if they were eggs. Then he tucked the newsprint over them and fitted the lid on top.

He held out the box. "Write."

This part was my job. I pulled a laundry marker from behind my ear and wrote "*J. Watson*" on the end of the box, and then the date: "*5/8/48*." I stacked the box on a shelf with the others that were waiting to be picked up.

"I don't mind doing it, Pop, but why not write on the boxes yourself?"

"You have the nice school handwriting," he said, patting my cheek like I was a little kid. (I hate that.) "My handwriting, it looks . . . like the immigrant's."

"So what if you're an immigrant? Your customers don't mind. Do they?"

Pop scribbled on the job ticket and added it to the spindle on his worktable. "Mind? Lots of them, they're the immigrants too. But we are all Americans now. My customers, they could go to any hat shop in town. But I want them to come to *my* shop. Your handwriting looks . . . what? Spiffy, *neh*? American." He reached out to pat my cheek again, but I dodged out of the way just in time.

The bell jingled on the door.

"Customer," said Pop, pulling the next pair of shoes off the shelf.

But it wasn't a customer. It was only Ace.

"Well?" he said. "Did you get sprung?"

"Three o'clock, okay? If no one comes in."

"Then hurry up and lock the door." If you knew Ace like I do, you'd know he wasn't kidding.

Just then, the bell jingled again. A man stood in the doorway, wearing an overcoat and hat.

"Too late," I told Ace. I nudged past him to greet the customer, just like Pop taught me. "How can I help you, sir?"

"Well, son, I need a pair of shoelaces toot sweet," said the man as he stepped into the quiet of the shop. He wasn't a regular customer. I'd never seen him before. He limped a little—as if an invisible small dog had latched on to his ankle and wouldn't let go.

"Sure thing. What color?" I reached behind the counter and pulled out a box of assorted laces.

"I suppose they ought to be brown, seeing as my shoes are brown." He leaned on the counter, wiggled his eyebrows, and grinned.

It was a corny thing to say, but I couldn't help smiling. I found a pair of waxed brown laces. "That'll be five cents."

The customer fished in a pocket and handed me a nickel. "Nice place you got here," he said, looking around.

"Thanks." But the shop was nothing fancy. A long, narrow room. Glass-fronted cases filled with men's hats for sale. Fedoras and homburgs, mostly. Some panamas. Even a few straw boaters. Behind the cases stood tall, open shelves of dark wood, stacked with boxes. Just inside the door, across from the cash register, was the shoe-shine stand, with three leather chairs on a raised platform. Right now, Ace was sprawled in one of them, digging dirt from under his fingernails. At the back of the shop, my pop was still bent over his worktable.

"I say, son, how much?"

"Huh?"

"A shoe shine," said the customer. "How much?"

"Oh. Twenty cents."

"Sign me up!"

"Sure thing. Pop! Shine!" Shining shoes was another one of my jobs, but Pop liked to meet the new customers and wait on them personally.

He got up from his workbench, smiling. Pop always has a smile on his face, even while he's sleeping. I've checked.

"Welcome, sir, good afternoon," said Pop, motioning toward the shoe-shine chairs with one hand and shooing Ace off with the other. The customer dropped his coat and hat on Ace's chair and settled in to the middle one.

Ace tugged at my elbow and tilted his head toward the door. "The fellas are waiting," he hissed.

I shook my head, but he yanked on my arm again, so I tried one more time. "Hey, Pop? You don't suppose . . ."

But Pop was already deep in conversation and shoe polish.

I wasn't going anywhere. As usual.

CHAPTER

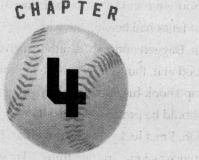

*S*EEMS LIKE A NICE TOWN," said the customer. He planted his feet on the brass footrests and extended a hand. "The name's Joe Daggett."

"Nice to meet you, Mister Daggett," said Pop. "I'm George Spirakis, and this is my son, Nikko."

"Nick." I stepped forward to shake Mr. Daggett's hand. And that's when I noticed that he was wearing only one sock. And that the ankle without a sock was made of wood.

But I didn't say anything. I didn't want to be impolite.

"You can call me Ace," said Ace, pushing his way into the group. Then he said, "Holy cow, a wooden leg!"

Pop and I both glared at him. But Mr. Daggett said, "It's all right, I don't mind. Take a look, fellas." He hitched up his trouser leg to just below his knee. The wooden part had leather straps that disappeared into his pant leg.

"You were in the war," said Pop. It was an easy guess. Lots of fellas had been in the war.

Mr. Daggett nodded. "Gunnery private in the Pacific. Not too good at it, though. Shot myself in the foot."

Pop shook his shoe-shine brush at him. "You joke, but you should be proud. You are a hero."

"Oh, I'm a lucky guy, I know that. Every pair of argyles lasts twice as long, for one thing." He grinned and wiggled his eyebrows, and I relaxed.

"So, Mister Daggett," said Pop, "you are in town on business?"

"That's right," said Joe Daggett, rolling down his trouser leg. "I'm in sales, you might say. Joining a little enterprise over at Eighth and Chalmers."

"Eighth and Chalmers," repeated Pop. "That's near the ballpark, *neh*?"

"Spittin' distance," said Joe Daggett. "Looking forward to taking in a game or two when I have the chance. You a Mudpuppies fan, George?"

"Everybody likes the baseball," said Pop, dipping a stiff brush into a tin of shoe polish. "My wife and I used to go. But Orchard Field, it's falling down. No place for a lady anymore. I read in the newspaper that the team is for sale. Going to fold up their tent stakes and leave town."

Pop never could quite get the hang of American slang.

"For sale?" said Joe Daggett. "Is that right?" He turned to me and Ace. "How about you fellas? Do you follow the Pups?"

"Not really," I said. I hated to disappoint him, because he seemed really excited about seeing some baseball. But the Mudpuppies had finished in the cellar of the Great Lakes League the last three seasons, and so far this year, they weren't looking any better.

"The Pups? They stink!" said Ace. "Not a single one of 'em is good enough to be a batboy, much less a ballplayer. Heck, even Nick here is a better right fielder than . . . what's his name?"

"Eddie . . . something," I said.

"Eddie Mulligan," said Joe Daggett, scratching his knee. "So you fellas are pretty good ballplayers, are ya?"

I said, "Sort of."

Ace said, "You bet we are!"

"Wish you could show those Mudpuppies a thing or two about how it's done, I suppose?"

"Darn tootin'!" said Ace. "Plenty of kids would love the chance to put on a Mudpuppies uniform, ain't that right, Nick?" He slapped me on the back.

All I said was, "Ow."

"You never know," said Joe Daggett. "Maybe one of these days you'll get your wish." He turned to Pop. "Say,

George, tell me a bit about yourself. What kind of name is Spirakis, anyway?"

"Greek," said Pop, sitting up straighter. "I was born there."

"How long you been in the States?"

Ace pulled the shop door open. "This is where I go play ball. See ya later, Nick." And he was gone, out into the sunshine.

"See ya," I grumbled.

Pop paid no attention. "I come to America when I was twelve years old. Same age my Nikko is right now." Pop beamed at me over his shoulder, as if I was the smartest kid in the world for figuring out how to turn twelve.

"And the rest of your family?" said Joe Daggett. Either he was very polite, or he was a really good salesman.

"My father, he sail here first, and then he send for me and my mother. My brother was born here. My father worked hard so he could buy this shop. He taught me the business, and now the shop is mine."

"How about your little brother?" said Joe Daggett, looking around. "Is he part of the family business?"

"Spiro?" said Pop, and for the first time his smile faded. "He's too busy having the fun. Out all night. Sleeps all day. *My* son will be different. Nicky is a good boy. He works hard too. And one day"—Pop spread his arms wide—"this shop, it will belong to him."

I shifted on my feet and smiled weakly at Joe Daggett.

Joe Daggett gave me a quick wink and changed the subject. "We all come from someplace else, ain't that the truth? My own folks are German and Irish. Which makes me Germish, I suppose. And what's wrong with that?" said Joe Daggett. "Not a thing."

"No sir, not a thing," echoed Pop as he buffed Joe Daggett's shoes to a high shine. "I am proud to be Greek. You are proud to be the Germish. And we are all proud to be American." He snapped his buffing cloth with a flourish. "Finished."

"Looks swell, George," said Joe Daggett, inspecting his shoes. He stepped down from the chair and gathered his coat and hat. "I'm glad I stopped in. What did you say this sleight of hand will set me back?"

Pop blinked up at Mr. Daggett, smiling and frowning at the same time.

"Twenty cents," I said.

"That's right," said Pop, relaxing and resting his hand on my shoulder. "Very nice to meet you, Mister Daggett. I wish you luck in your business."

"Why, thanks, George," said Joe Daggett, handing Pop two dimes and a business card. "Next time you're near Eighth and Chalmers, look me up. My door is always open." Then he searched his coat pockets. "Here you go, Nick. Compliments of the Mudpuppies."

He plopped a brand new baseball into my hand, and limped out of the shop, to a jangle of bells.

"How about that?" said Pop, showing me the card. "The Mudpuppies are not for sale anymore."

My mouth fell open when I read the card. "Jeepers. We just met the new owner of the Mudpuppies!"

CHAPTER

5

"COME NOW, NICK." Mrs. Dimitropoulos was hanging over my shoulder in a cloud of old-lady perfume. "You remember your Greek alphabet, don't you? Sound out the letters."

I chewed my pencil and stared at the blank work sheet on my desk. I'd been speaking Greek all my life, but on paper it was *hard*. For one thing, the Greek alphabet has only twenty-four letters, and they all look like meaningless squiggles. What the heck happened to two whole letters? I was never a good speller to begin with, and now I was supposed to do it using squiggles, and without two of the letters?

Plus, I was sleepy. And hungry. It's the same thing every Tuesday: Spend the whole day in school, stop home for a snack, and then take the streetcar to Greek school. Sit in the church basement for two hours with the priest's wife telling you to sound out the letters (as if that's all there is to it). And when it's finally done, ride the streetcar home again, in the dark. Choke down your cold supper so you can start on your regular homework.

Did anyone ask me if I *wanted* to go to Greek school? No.

Right now, all the other kids were bent over their own papers. Most of them had sickly looks on their faces, which would've been funny, except my own face probably looked the same. A few kids (mostly girls) were breezing right along. Just like in regular school. Could I help it if I liked numbers better? Batting averages, ERAs, win-loss records. Important, real-world stuff.

I scrawled my name in Greek at the top of my paper. At least I remembered that much. It was enough to make Mrs. D. decide to go torture someone else.

I couldn't stop thinking about Joe Daggett. The new owner of the Mudpuppies! And me and Ace spouting off about how awful the Pups were. But Joe Daggett had given me an official Mudpuppies baseball, so he couldn't have been too mad, could he?

I felt a poke between my shoulder blades. It was Pete, holding out a crumpled scrap of paper.

You remember Pete. Me and him went way back, and let's just say we weren't exactly best friends. In fact, we hated each other's guts. Sure, we played ball together (you do what you gotta do, to keep a Scramble team going), and we lived four blocks apart, but other than that, we didn't have much in common. Except being Greek. So, even though he was a show-off and a big mouth and a knucklehead who beat me up at least once a week from kindergarten till second grade, me and Pete were stuck going to Greek school together.

I grabbed the scrap of paper and turned around again, dropping my hand into my lap in case Mrs. D. noticed. When the coast was clear, I peeked at the paper. It said:

#6???

I turned and gave him a puzzled look.

"Question number six," hissed Pete, leaning across his desk and shooting a glance toward Mrs. D. "What's the answer?"

I should mention here that probably the only reason Pete passed second grade was because he copied off me for most of that year. But things had changed since second grade.

"I don't know," I whispered back. "Something about buying squash at the market."

"Squash?" He looked down at his paper and scratched his head. "I thought it said watermelon."

"I don't know, Pete," I whispered. "Do it yourself."

He snatched the note back. "Wait'll the next time you're in right field," he muttered. "I'm gonna clobber that ball over the fence again."

I knew it! Did I mention that I hate Pete's guts?

"Boys," called Mrs. D. from the front of the room. "Do your own work, please."

I turned around, but after a few seconds I got another poke in the back, and another note.

#8???

I couldn't help it. I turned around and said, "Cut it out, Pete!"

"Boys!"

It could have been worse. We could have been hauled off to see the priest, who would have told our folks, who would have given me all kinds of grief. I could hear them now: *How you could embarrass us like that, don't you know how hard that poor woman works to teach you something, you should be proud of your heritage, instead you act like the hooligans and goat herders.* Never mind that back in Greece, our family *had* been goat herders, and besides, what did that have to do with being a hooligan? But I knew that wasn't the point. It was the embarrassment part.

Instead, we got extra homework.

As we rode the streetcar home, Pete said, "Let's do it together." He really meant, "Let me copy off you."

"Sorry," I said, even though I wasn't. I held my work sheet next to Pete's. "They're different assignments."

"What?" Pete slouched on the seat. "That Mrs. D. sure is sneaky. My folks won't help me either."

I folded my work sheet and jammed it into my back pocket. "I might be able to get my ma to help me. That way she can learn to read English at the same time."

"Your ma can't read English?"

"Not too well," I said. "She didn't come to the States until she was sixteen. She never went to American school."

This is what I mean about being Greek. I couldn't admit that kind of thing to just anyone—not even to Ace. But Pete's folks were born in Greece too, so he knows what it's like. He just said, "What happens when you bring a note home from school? Like when you get in trouble and stuff?"

I shrugged. Sure, I got in trouble at school sometimes, but nothing big. Talking in class. Forgetting my homework. Not exactly Pete-caliber trouble. "I read 'em to my ma," I said. "What else?" She never exactly punished me, anyway. Usually she just made me promise to try harder.

"Holy moly." Pete pulled the signal cord. "You got a lot

of guts. My ma never even sees the notes I bring home." The streetcar squealed to a stop, and we hopped off.

"I don't get it," I said as we started down the sidewalk. "How do you get her to sign a note she never sees?"

Pete clapped me on the back. "You got a lot to learn, pal. I been forging my ma's signature since third grade."

$\mathcal{A}$FTER SCHOOL THE NEXT DAY, Ace was waiting for me in our usual spot at the edge of the playground.

"What's the score?" I asked him as we pushed our way through the crowds of kids on the way home from school. We were headed to the zoo to pick up the Scramble game where the guys had left off the day before. (I'd missed yesterday on account of Greek school.)

"We're ahead, nine to seven," Ace told me as we walked down the sidewalk. "And no run-ins with Tank."

"That's 'cause Pete wasn't there. If he hits the ball over the fence again, he can get it himself. Let's see how *he* likes Tank breathing down his neck."

"At least now we have another baseball," said Ace. "Good ol' Joe Daggett. The fellas still don't believe that we met the Mudpuppies' owner. They think you bought that ball."

I laughed. "Where would I get ninety-eight cents for a new baseball? That's three weeks' worth of tip money."

We got out our mitts and started playing catch as we walked down the sidewalk. Whenever we passed a group of kids, we tossed the ball over their heads. This might sound like trouble, but we do it all the time, and we hardly ever hit anyone.

Right now we had to get around a passel of fifth-grade girls, so Ace went wide left and I went wide right. I tossed the ball up and over the girls in a perfect arc. Ace reached for it with his glove—

—and a hand shot up from the middle of the herd of girls and grabbed the ball out of midair.

The girls squealed and scattered, leaving one girl standing alone on the sidewalk. She was taller than the others, with scuffed saddle shoes and this huge cloud of black hair. One hand rested a stack of books on her hip, and the other hand was holding *my* baseball. She stared at me and chomped her gum.

"Hey." I held out my hand. "That's mine."

She squinted at me. She blew a bubble. She was taller than me. I hate that. She did *not* hand me back my ball. She just set down her books and said, "Go long."

"Huh?"

But she didn't say anything else. She looked up the street. She looked down the street. She watched a coal truck rumble past. And then she wound up like she was Joe DiMaggio in center field.

"Go long!" yelled Ace, as we both realized what was happening. We took off across the street just as she heaved the ball high into the air.

I went charging after it, almost tripping over the curb, and plowed through a bunch of kindergartners like they were bowling pins. Little kids were crying, bigger kids were hollering, and that ball came whistling down from the sky like a comet.

What did I do?

I froze.

Because—as you might recall—I can't catch a fly ball to save my life.

There I was, chasing after a ball thrown by a *girl*, and everyone was watching me, and I was going to miss it.

And sure enough, it went sailing over my head. My brand-new, official Mudpuppies baseball, headed for the storm sewer and Lake Michigan.

THUNK!

"Got it!"

I whirled around. It was Ace, right behind me, with his mitt in the air and the ball in his mitt. The kindergartners all stopped crying and gave him a round of applause.

In fact, so many kids were gathering around Ace on one side of the street, and around that tall girl on the other side, that no one seemed to notice my pathetic performance. Which was fine by me.

"Did you see the arm on that girl?" I overheard one kid saying.

"I seen *both* her arms," said some other kid. "Long and hairy. Did she escape from the monkey house at the zoo, or what?"

I looked across the street at the tall girl. She did have a lot of hair. There was some kind of ribbon tied around her head, but it wasn't doing much to hold things back. And her arms *were* long, but so were her legs, and all the rest of her.

She didn't seem like a person who needed someone else to stick up for her. And she hadn't exactly done me any favors by humiliating me in front of everybody (with *my* baseball, no less). But that wasn't the point. The point was, making fun of a person because they can't catch a ball thrown by a girl is one thing. But a person can't do anything about the length of their arms.

I searched around for the kid who'd made the crack about monkeys. There he was: some scrawny fifth grader with an expression that made you wonder if he ate nothing but pickles.

"Hey, kid," I told him. "Pick on someone your own size,

why don't ya. Oh, right, you can't, 'cause there's no one else around here who's a rat!"

I grabbed my baseball out of Ace's glove and stalked away, leaving the kid standing there with his sourpuss mouth hanging open.

Behind me, the kindergartners were laughing.

CHAPTER

*A*CE CAUGHT UP WITH ME, and we walked six blocks without saying a word.

Well, *I* didn't say a word.

"Did you see the look on that kid's face?" said Ace. "You really shut him up! Can you believe the arm on that girl? Where'd she learn to throw like that? Did you see how I caught the ball? Just like Joltin' Joe. Do you think I looked like Joltin' Joe?"

For six blocks.

When we got to Forty-Seventh Street, I tugged his elbow. "Let's go the long way. I need to blow off some steam."

So instead of cutting through the park toward the Scramble field as usual, we turned to walk down Forty-Seventh Street, and around the edge of the park.

To be honest, I liked going the long way. You learn in school that the Earth is divided in half at the equator, but if you ask me, that's wrong. The Earth is divided in half right where I was standing.

And here's why: On one side of the street there's a typical busy, noisy city. Houses, schools, factories, churches; butcher shops, barber shops, the brewery; cars honking, busses belching, and streetcars squealing.

But on the other side of Forty-Seventh Street, everything changes. For one thing, there's a big, peaceful park. Acres and acres of grass and trees. Walking paths, tennis courts, a pond and boathouse; a band shell with a dance pavilion. A sledding hill. And, as I've already mentioned, a zoo. Tigers and lions. Giraffes, buffaloes, hippos. Polar bears, brown bears, grizzly bears. One lonesome elephant. A stumpy-legged rhinoceros patrolling the right-field fence. A gazillion monkeys.

How did all those animals end up here, anyway? I can just imagine the zoo hunter: *Excuse me, Mister Giraffe* (for example). *How'd you like to leave this nice, warm African grassland and come to a city in the upper Midwest of the USA, and spend the rest of your life in a pen the size of my living room? You'll have a nifty view of the Number 37 streetcar line, and in the winter you can play in the snow! What's snow, you ask? Come on into this nice cozy crate here and I'll show you.*

That's probably not what actually happened. But if

Mister Giraffe could talk, I bet that's pretty much how he'd tell it. Anyhow, I'm grateful, because sure as shootin' I'll never make it to Africa or Ceylon or anywhere like that, so all those animals have done me a big favor. Because here I am, with a regular Noah's Ark only three blocks from my house.

Ace and I walked down Forty-Seventh Street now, past the bear dens and the elephant yard. It was still off-season at the zoo, so most of the animals were hunkered down inside their winter quarters. But the polar bears were out, of course. And around the corner, along Frederick Street, the mountain goats were out too. And so was Tank.

Behind Tank's yard, Monkey Island sat deserted and silent. The empty tire swing dangled from the branch of a huge dead tree. The water in the moat looked as smooth and black as slate.

"I can't wait till they let the monkeys out," said Ace. "It's just like the last day of school. All those monkeys busting out into the open. They look so happy."

Ace was right. The day Monkey Island reopens is a big deal, and not just for the monkeys. Practically the whole city comes to watch as all the zoo animals are officially allowed outside for the summer. There's a parade, and a brass band, and free ice cream. I never miss it. But I almost like the winter zoo better, when we have the place—and the animals—pretty much to ourselves.

As soon as we caught sight of the fellas at the ball field, they started hollering for us.

"Look at this!" said Charlie, waving a newspaper. As we got closer, I saw the headline:

NEW PUPS OWNER ITCHING
TO SHAKE THINGS UP
EXCITEMENT IN STORE FOR THE '48 SEASON

"Somebody left this paper on the park bench," said Charlie. "And I saw the headline. The Mudpuppies are having a contest!"

CHAPTER 8

*W*HAT KIND OF CONTEST?" said Ace.

"It's a contest for kids!" said Chuck. "That's us!"

Good ol' Chuck, master of the obvious.

Pete gave Charlie a shove. "Go on, professor. Read the whole thing."

Charlie pushed up his glasses and read the article out loud:

> "Joseph P. Daggett, new president and general
> manager of our own Mudpuppies Baseball Club, has
> hit the ground running. Daggett announced exciting
> doings at the Ol' Orchard, including Ladies' Days,
> surprise giveaways, and a special contest just for
> kids, with a grand prize to be awarded during an

upcoming home stand. 'I hope everybody comes out this season and has a swell time at the ballpark,' said Daggett, who took the helm just last week. 'I want Orchard Field, and our team, to be something all the fans can be proud of.'

"Will our perennial cellar dwellers finally field a winning team? Our hopes are up! Good luck, President Daggett and the entire Mudpuppies organization."

"My pop was over by the ballpark yesterday," said Chuck. "He told me there was a crew painting the whole place. Really spiffing it up, my ol' man said."

Ace nudged me and said into my ear, "Remember how your pop told Joe Daggett that the Orchard was falling apart?"

I nodded. "And no place for a lady. He's using our ideas!"

"Get to the good stuff already," Pete was telling Charlie. "What's the special contest for kids? Keep reading."

"That's the whole article," said Charlie. "But look at this." He flipped the page to show us a full-page ad:

> **BOYS!**
> **ARE YOU AGED 10 TO 14?**
> **DO YOU LOVE BASEBALL?**
> **NOW'S YOUR CHANCE TO BE**
> **MUDPUPPY FOR A DAY!***

THE MUDPUPPIES BASEBALL CLUB
ANNOUNCES THE FIRST ANNUAL MUDPUPPY
FOR A DAY BATBOY CONTEST. WEAR THE
OFFICIAL TEAM UNIFORM ON THE FIELD!
JOIN THE PLAYERS IN THE DUGOUT! TAR
AND ROSIN THE BATS OF YOUR HOMETOWN
HEROES! FILL THOSE WATER JUGS!

DO YOU HAVE WHAT IT TAKES?

*SEE TERMS AND CONDITIONS

Below this was an entry form, with blank spaces for name and address and stuff like that. Then there were a couple of paragraphs of really small printing.

Charlie scanned the fine print while all the fellas gathered around. "Here's the details. Let's see . . ."

"Hurry up and read it already!"

Charlie cleared his throat. "'Boys aged ten to fourteen . . .'"

The fellas voiced their encouragement. "Yeah, yeah, we know that. What else?"

"Gimme a chance here! 'All entrants must compete in two categories. Category One: Field Skills . . .'"

"Now you're talking!" said Chuck.

"I could whip any of you punks, any day!" said Pete.

"We'll see about that," said Ace.

"'Category Two . . . ,'" read Charlie, stepping between Ace and Pete. "'A written essay of one hundred words or fewer, explaining why you should be Mudpuppy for a Day.'"

If it's possible for time to stand still, that's what happened then. For five heartbeats at least, there was complete silence. You could've heard a mouse burp.

Then clocks started ticking again and Pete snatched the newspaper out of Charlie's hands. "Let me see that." He glared at the paper, like he was daring the blobs of ink to be arranged the way Charlie had read them. Then he smacked Charlie on the chest with the folded-up paper. "It's a stupid contest."

"What's the matter, Pete?" said Ace. "You afraid of a hundred words? Maybe you wanna bow out now, before you embarrass yourself." It's times like this when I wondered if Ace actually *wanted* to get punched.

But Pete just said, "You wish, you little toad." And he stalked off, taking the newspaper with him. Dollars to donuts he was going home to fill out that contest entry form.

"How hard can it be to write a hundred words?" said Charlie. "That's like . . . writing a thank-you letter to your grandma."

"Yeah," I said, but my voice was a little wobbly. Writing is not my best subject.

Then again, it's not as bad as my fielding.

Holy smokes. I was in trouble.

"Hey! We gotta _practice!_" said Ace, already forgetting about Pete. "What kind of skills do you suppose they'll wanna see? Hitting, I guess. And fielding." He slapped me on the back. "I'll help you work on that one, buddy."

"Gee, thanks." Did I mention I was in trouble?

But what could I do? I couldn't NOT enter the contest. That would be admitting defeat, which is somehow even worse than public humiliation. Besides, who's to say I couldn't win this contest? None of the other fellas was any great shakes at writing either (except maybe Charlie, who seemed to think that delivering newspapers made him a literary genius). And sure, I was a lousy outfielder, but I could hold my own at the other stuff: hitting, base running. Okay, so I had a snowball's chance of winning this contest, but it was a chance. And that's all I needed: one chance.

For some reason, nobody wanted to play ball anymore. Everybody wandered off, no doubt to find their own copies of the paper.

Me and Ace looked at each other.

"I guess I'll just go home, then," I said.

"Me too," said Ace.

"Newspaper's probably already sitting on the front porch."

"Yep." And then he took off like a shot. I followed him.

We raced the entire two blocks home. Sure enough, the

newspaper had already been delivered. We each ran up our porch steps, scooped up our newspapers, and tossed aside all but the Sports section.

There it was, on the back page.

The entry form was blank and clean, just waiting to be filled out. I scanned it quick, breathing hard from the race home. Sure enough, just like Charlie had read: "Fill out the entry form (name, age, address, parent signature, etc.). Bring the form and your essay to Orchard Field on the day of the field skills contest, Saturday, May 22."

"Wait a minute," I squeaked. "Saturday?"

CHAPTER

9

I LOOKED OVER TOWARD Ace's front porch, but he was gone. So I ran next door and leaned on the buzzer. When the door opened, an invisible cloud of fried liver and onions hit me in the face. I forced myself not to stagger backward.

"Nick!" It was Ace's ma, in a flowery housecoat. Her hair was done up in curlers, and anyone who looked at her could tell where Ace got his ears. "Is something wrong, dear? You're all out of breath."

I shut my mouth and shook my head. The more I talked, the more liver and onion I'd get up my nose.

"I suppose you're looking for Horace," said Ace's ma. "I thought I heard him come in a minute ago—"

That's when Ace came barreling past her out the door

and kept going. "See ya later, Ma!" he called over his shoulder. "Nick invited me for supper." He clattered down the porch steps and cut across the lawn to my house.

"Oh," said Ace's ma. "Isn't that nice of you, Nick. Tell your family hello for me, will you? Your mother was so kind to weed our front lawn the other day. Not a dandelion in sight anymore!"

"Sure thing, Mrs. P." I escaped down the steps and followed Ace to my front porch.

"When did I invite you for supper?" I asked him.

"Please?" said Ace, plopping down onto the top step. "Did you catch a whiff of what's going on over at my house? Hey, look!" He pulled the torn newspaper page out of his back pocket and unfolded it. "We can fill 'em out tonight."

I sank down next to him. "Did you read the whole thing?"

He frowned and studied the page. "'Field skills contest, Saturday, May 22.' That's swell! That means we'll have plenty of time to—wait a minute. Saturday?"

I groaned. "Now what am I gonna do? My pop will never let me off work." My own newspaper sat on the porch like a dead fish. I gave it a halfhearted kick.

"Couldn't you at least ask?" said Ace. "He almost let you play ball last Saturday. Maybe, once he knows what a big deal it is—"

I shook my head. "I dunno. Pop always says the only thing more important than work is school."

"Then tell 'em there's a field trip, maybe."

"What kind of field trip is on a Saturday?"

Ace shrugged. "A trip to the state capitol or something?"

"All the way to Madison? Not even my folks would buy a story like that." I scuffed at a weed sprouting through a crack in the walk.

"You'd better figure something out," said Ace. "It wouldn't be any fun without you. Besides, if you don't do the contest, Pete will say it's 'cause you're scared of him."

"Pete doesn't scare me."

"Don't tell *him* that. He'll try to change your mind in a hurry."

"Oh, hi," said a voice.

There on the sidewalk, on a bicycle that was too big for her, was that girl. The tall girl with all the hair, who almost threw my brand-new baseball into the storm sewer.

"Do you live here?" she said.

"No," I told her. "We're just hangin' around till somebody offers to adopt us." Because I was still pretty sore about the baseball incident.

"You're Nick, right? And Ace?"

I squinted at her. "How'd you know that?"

She shrugged like it was obvious. "I've seen you around

school. I'm Penny Lonergan. I live two blocks over. We moved here from Kenosha during Easter vacation. My dad got a job at the brewery. I'm exploring the neighborhood. Nice catch, by the way." Now she was talking to Ace, of course.

"Thanks," said Ace, sitting up straighter. "Nice throw." He grinned like a fool.

"Thanks," she said. She blew a bubble.

"Where'd you learn to throw like that, anyway?" I said.

"My sister," said the girl, with a completely straight face. She pointed at the torn newspaper page in Ace's hand. "What ya got there?" And without even being invited, she dropped her bike onto the sidewalk, sauntered up *my* front walk, and sat herself down on the porch step, right next to me and Ace.

She leaned over and peeked at the page. "A contest! You guys gonna enter?"

"Maybe," I said. As if it was any of her business, anyway.

"You bet we're gonna enter," said Ace. "And one of us is gonna win, too."

"Do you know a kid named Pete?" said Penny. "I heard him say that *he* was gonna win some kind of contest."

"Is that so?" said Ace.

"He seemed pretty sure about it."

"There's something you should know about Pete," I told her.

"Oh, I've met him. On my first day at school, he told me that new kids have to give him the cookies out of their lunch bag."

"That stinks," I told her. Even though I was still sore at her.

"It's all right," she said with a shrug. "It only happened once. I guess he didn't like a wad of chewed bubblegum stuck between two Fig Newtons." She grinned and blew a bubble. "Well, I gotta get home. See ya around." And then she sauntered back to her bike and rode away down the street.

"How do ya like that?" said Ace, watching her go. "A girl who's not afraid to stand up to Pete."

"She doesn't know Pete like we do," I said. "Nobody does something like that to Pete and gets away with it."

The screen door squeaked open behind us. "Nicky, you're home?"

"Hiya, Ma."

"Supper is ready," she said. "Hello, Azy."

"Hiya, Mrs. S. Can I stay for supper?"

She cocked an eyebrow at Ace. "You like *fassoulada*?"

Ace leaned toward me and whispered, "Do I?"

"Bean soup," I told him.

Ace thought about it for a second. Then he said to Ma, "It's my favorite."

"Good boy," said Ma. "Come wash up." And she disappeared again into the house.

I looked over at Ace. "*Do* you like bean soup?"

"Never had it," he admitted. "But anything's better than liver and onions."

CHAPTER 10

A NSWER ME, SPIRO!" Pop was hollering as we walked into the kitchen. He shook a finger and glared at my uncle, who was a younger, taller version of Pop. "How you will make something of yourself if you sleep every day until three o'clock?"

Uncle Spiro waved him off. "I'll be fine, George. Don't worry about me."

Imagine that half of this conversation is being hollered in Greek. That's the way things go at my house. But to make it easier, I've translated it all into English.

"Everybody! Sit down!" commanded Ma. She was even smaller than Pop, but her voice was bigger. "Nicky, bring the milk from the icebox, *neh*?"

I grabbed the milk bottle from the fridge and set it on the table.

"Something sure smells good, Mrs. S.," said Ace, as if he didn't even hear all the hollering.

Ma and Pop are always hollering. They're not mad, usually. It's just that their volume is stuck on LOUD. To them, nothing is worth talking about if you can't argue about it. *The weather, it's so hot today!* Pop might say. Then Ma goes, *Hot? Are you crazy? It was hotter yesterday!* When Spiro's around, Pop hollers at him instead of at Ma. I figure that's why she hasn't kicked Spiro out of the house yet. Nobody hollers at me much, as long as they have each other to holler at. That's fine by me.

Uncle Spiro sat down and shook out his napkin. "Well, if it isn't good ol' Ace! I haven't seen you since you were a little squirt!"

"Gee whiz, Spiro," said Ace, with his goofy grin. "You see me all the time."

"Oh, right," said Spiro. "That means you're still a little squirt!"

Ace nodded agreeably as he pulled up an extra chair. Nobody but Uncle Spiro could get away with teasing Ace like that.

"Hiya, *thio*," I said to my uncle, pouring milk for me and Ace.

"What's shakin', Nikko?" Spiro rubbed my crew cut.

Ma pushed between us with a bowl of hot soup. "Eat!" she ordered, and went back to the stove to fill more bowls from a gigantic pot. Finally, she untied her apron, wiped her red face with it, and sat down with the rest of us.

We'd barely lifted our spoons when Pop started again. "When you are going to get a job?"

I decided to make my move, on the chance that Pop was too busy hollering at Spiro to notice himself giving me the day off next Saturday. "I brought the paper inside for you, Pop. Did you know that sometimes there's contests announced in the paper?"

Ace gave me an encouraging nod as he stirred his soup.

"Is that so?" said Uncle Spiro, seeing his chance to change the subject. "Say, does your buddy Charlie still have that morning paper route?"

"Only on the weekends," I said.

"Yeah," said Ace. "On school days he needs his beauty sleep."

"Why you sleep until three o'clock every day?" demanded Pop.

Uncle Spiro blew on his spoon. "I told you, George," he said patiently, "I have night school." He slurped his soup. "Delicious, Athena. You should open a restaurant."

Ma beamed.

"You are twenty-five years old," said Pop. "Too old for school. You have a good job waiting for you in the shop."

"But I *want* to go to school," said Uncle Spiro. He never hollers. It drives Pop bonkers. "And the GI Bill is paying for it, so like I said. You don't have to worry. Pass the bread, please."

I slid the bread plate across to Spiro, who gave me a wink.

Pop jabbed his spoon into his soup. He finally took a bite, and his scowl melted into his usual contented grin. "The best soup in the world, Athena." He leaned over and kissed Ma on the cheek.

Ma blushed with pride. It's funny: no matter how much my family hollers at each other, they never argue about food.

"What kind of school is this anyway, that you come home so late every night?"

Spiro didn't answer. He just dipped a chunk of bread into his soup.

"You need to learn the useful things," Pop said, shaking his spoon.

Uncle Spiro tore off another chunk of bread. "What's useful, George? Blocking hats? Shining shoes? What if I want something different?"

I knew how he felt.

I tried again. "Could I have the day off from the shop next Saturday, Pop? For the contest at the ballpark?"

But he was glaring at Uncle Spiro. "The shop is not

good enough for you? It's good enough to pay for this food you eat, this roof you sleep under. It's good enough for me. Good enough for Nicky. Why not for you?"

A mouthful of scalding soup caught in my throat. My eyes watered from the heat as I gulped it down.

Ace pushed a glass of milk toward me.

"Don't bring Nicky into this," said Spiro, and I took a grateful swallow of cold milk. "Nicky's just a kid. He doesn't know what he wants."

The milk went down wrong. I sputtered into my napkin.

Ma dropped her spoon with a clatter and started smacking me on the back.

I waved her off. "Pop!" I hollered. "I need the day off work next Saturday!"

But here's what happens when you're part of a family that hollers all the time: When *you* start hollering, nobody notices.

"I am older than you, Spiro," said Pop. The veins on his forehead were sticking out. "I already make something of myself. I know about the world!"

"The world?" said Spiro, his voice finally rising too. "You grew up in a tiny village with no running water and more goats than people!" He lifted his chin. "I've seen plenty of the world. I was in the war. I was on the front lines in France!"

Pop threw his napkin onto the table. "You were a cook!"

"I was still there," said Uncle Spiro. His voice was low and level again, but it could have sliced iron.

The two brothers glared at each other, jaws clenched, nostrils flaring.

Ace lifted his bowl and smacked his lips. "Could I please have some more soup?"

CHAPTER 11

I SCRAPED MY CHAIR BACKWARD. "Thanks for supper, Ma. We're going over to Ace's to do homework."

Ace's mouth dropped open. "But I wanted—"

Uncle Spiro stood too. "I'm late for school." He pecked Ma on the cheek, grabbed the car keys from their hook, and banged out the back door.

Ma threw up her hands. "Why he always forgets his jacket? Nicky, be a good boy and wear your jacket, *neh*? You'll catch a cold!"

"I'm only going next door, Ma." I escaped to the front hall. As I was putting on my ball cap, Ace busted out from the kitchen, waving his napkin.

"What's the matter with you?" he said. "I wasn't finished!"

"You can have more soup later. Are you coming?" I pushed out the front door and onto the porch.

Ace followed me out. "Where?" Then he gasped. "You don't really wanna do homework, do you?"

"Did you hear them? *Nicky's just a kid. Nicky doesn't know what he wants*. Like I wasn't even there!"

"My folks are the same way," said Ace. "When you want 'em to pay attention, they ignore you. But when you *don't* want them to—like when you accidentally bust a water balloon on your sister's head, for example—they won't leave you alone. I'm telling ya: you can't win."

"Why do I always have to do what my pop wants me to do, anyway?"

Ace leaned against the porch railing. "'Cause you're a kid?"

He was right. I hate that.

I paced across the front porch. In the distance, a lion roared. "He makes me work in the shop every Saturday. He makes me go to Greek school every Tuesday. He talks about being American, but he wants me to be exactly like him. All I want is one lousy Saturday off to do that Mudpuppy contest. Is that so much to ask?"

No, it wasn't.

"That's it," I said. "One way or another, I'm gonna be in that contest." I clattered down the steps and out to the sidewalk.

Ace whooped and hurried after me. "Now you're talking! Where are we going?"

"I dunno. Let's walk. I think better when I walk."

Out of habit, we headed toward the zoo. The sun was going down, and I kind of wished I'd brought my jacket. By the time we got to Frederick Street, my arms were covered with goose bumps.

"So," said Ace finally. "Any ideas for getting the day off?"

"Nope," I admitted.

"Try one more time to ask your Pop," he said. "You never know."

"You saw what it's like," I told him. "He doesn't even listen to me."

Then something caught Ace's eye. "Hey," he said, looking over my shoulder. "Isn't that your uncle?"

I turned to see a 1936 Nash cruise slowly past. It stopped at the corner of Forty-Third Street, and then turned right.

"Yep, that's Uncle Spiro," I said, checking the license plate. "He's going to night school."

"Isn't it that way? Toward downtown?" Ace pointed east along Frederick Street.

"Yeah . . ."

"Then why is he going *that* way?" Ace swept his arm around and pointed south.

I didn't have an answer. We dashed to the corner and watched the Nash as it drifted down Forty-Third Street toward the viaduct, until its taillights blurred in the twilight and blended with the other traffic on the bridge.

"What's that all about?" said Ace, finally. "Do ya think it has something to do with him getting home late, and sleeping till three in the afternoon?"

I shrugged. "He's probably just going to a filling station or something."

"There aren't any filling stations that way," said Ace. "It's all factories and stuff, and then the highway."

We stared after the car until a bus slid past, blocking our view down the street.

"So where do ya suppose he's going?" said Ace. Then he grinned and nudged me. "Maybe he's going to meet some girl."

I sighed and started for home. Above our heads, the streetlights switched on, one by one. "Just 'cause he's not going straight to school doesn't mean he's not *going* to school. Maybe he's picking up a friend from the south side of town."

"A *girl*friend." Ace snorted at his own joke.

"You're nuts," I told him. "My pop is already sore at Spiro for going to school. How sore do you think he'd be if Spiro wasn't going to school after all? And lying about it too?"

"Maybe that's why he's lying about it." Sometimes, Ace is too smart for his own good.

But it made me wonder. If Uncle Spiro *had* wanted to keep a secret from Pop, who could blame him? Then again, Spiro didn't need to keep any secrets from Pop. The nightly arguments were proof enough that he wasn't afraid to stand up to anybody.

We walked toward home in the dark. Frederick Street was clogged with traffic, but on the other side, beyond the glow of the headlights and the streetlights and the stoplights, the zoo was sleeping, dark and quiet. You'd never know it was there at all . . . unless, of course, you *did* know. It was as if the zoo held secrets of its own.

"So," said Ace, nudging me. "Are ya gonna tell your pop?"

"Nah." I didn't know what was going on with Uncle Spiro. But I knew one thing for sure. If Uncle Spiro had a secret, I wasn't going to be the one to tell it.

CHAPTER

12

ℳY MIND WAS MADE UP: I was going to enter that contest. But first, I needed Pop to sign the entry form.

When I walked in the front door, I could hear him in the kitchen, reading the paper.

We get both the morning and the evening newspapers at our house. That's two editions of the paper every day (except on Sundays), and Pop reads every word of every page. He takes the *Sentinel* with him in the morning and reads it on the streetcar or at the shop. Then, at night when Ma is cleaning up the supper dishes, he reads the *Journal*. He starts on the front page and doesn't stop until he squeezes out every bit of the three cents he paid for that paper. I mean, he reads everything: every ad, every comic (including the mushy ones, like *Mary Worth*), every high school sports score—the whole nine yards. Even the obituaries. I'm telling ya, a person can't die in this town without Pop trying to figure out their entire life from one short paragraph. *Look this man, Athena, he will be buried in the Wanderer's Rest. Same place as your mother! I wonder, is this the man who lived upstairs from her in 1932? The name, it looks familiar.*

Because here's another thing: Pop reads most of the paper out loud. Partly so Ma can get the news too, since (as I've mentioned) she's not too good at reading English. And partly so Pop can ask me to translate a tricky word here or there, or to explain the slang. The Sports page is the worst. I mean, he knows that stealing a base won't land a guy in jail. But when it comes to other stuff, it's a headache waiting to happen. *Nicky, why this player on the Mudpuppies is hitting a can of corn to the outfield? They don't have enough baseballs?* Stuff like that. And when you think about it, it *is* confusing. No wonder he gets his expressions mixed up sometimes. I just wish he wouldn't do it in public.

So anyway, I went back into the house and hung around, waiting for my chance to grab the Sports page. Ma and Pop were still in the kitchen, and from the sound of Pop's voice, I guessed that he hadn't gotten that far yet. The Sports section is the last section of the paper. Right now he was reading the advice column in the Green Sheet, which meant Sports was next.

"Listen to this, Athena," I could hear him saying. "'Dear Mrs. Gibbs: I have a nosy neighbor. She is always peeking into my windows at night while she is out walking her dog. What should I do? Signed, Fed Up.'"

I could hear Ma *tsk*ing, and the clink of dishes as she put them away in the cupboard. "Oh, those nosy neighbors, they are a problem. What does Mrs. Gibbs have to say?"

"Let's see . . ." The newspaper rattled, and I imagined Pop turning it to get more light. "Mrs. Gibbs, she says, 'Dear Fed: Close your drapes at night.'"

That did it. They both started laughing.

"Oh, Mrs. Gibbs. She always knows what to say."

The newspaper rattled again. Maybe Pop was finally turning to the Sports page.

"How about that?" I heard Pop saying. "Mister Joe Daggett is in the newspaper!"

Bingo.

I walked into the kitchen, all casual. "Hey, Pop, how's it goin'?"

"Nicky?" said Ma. "I thought you went to Azy's house to do the homework."

"Look, Nicky," said Pop. "Mister Daggett is in the paper. Athena, this is the man who came into the shop last Saturday. He's itching to shake things up for the Mudpuppies. See?" He tapped on the headline, one word at a time. "'Shake. Things. Up.'"

Ma smiled and nodded, and turned back to the sink. "That's nice."

"Mister Daggett is a very nice man," agreed Pop. He turned the page and launched into reading out the scores of a high school track meet. Apparently Washington High was the team to beat this season.

I picked up a dish towel and started in on the soup pot Ma had just finished scrubbing, trying to act like I wasn't hanging around. For my efforts, I got one cheek pinched and the other one kissed. "Gee whiz, Ma" was all I said, wiping my cheek with the towel.

After half of forever, Pop finally turned to the back page of the Sports section. "Look here, Nicky. A contest for boys, aged ten to fourteen. That Mister Daggett, he's a smart man. So many big ideas!"

I tossed the dish towel onto the drain board and hopped over next to Pop. "Mind if I take a look?"

"Sure, sure," said Pop, handing me the Sports section.

There it was: The contest entry form, all blank and perfect and waiting to be filled out.

"So, Pop," I said as casual as I could, "I was thinking of maybe entering this contest." It was worth another try.

"Good idea," said Pop, folding the rest of the paper and laying it on the kitchen table. "I know you can win. You are a very smart boy."

I gave him a hopeful smile. "Thanks, Pop. Say, uh, you

need a parent's signature, though." I showed him the form.

"Good for Mister Daggett," said Pop. "He respects the parents." He pulled his fountain pen out of his shirt pocket and uncapped it.

I held my breath.

The pen hovered over the blank form. "What is this?" said Pop. He adjusted his glasses and peered closer. "The contest is on a Saturday?"

"Oh, really?" I squeaked. "Well, uh, maybe just this one time—"

"Nicky. You know that Saturdays are working days. I need you in the shop." He capped his pen and held out the newspaper, unsigned. "There will be other contests, *neh*?"

I opened my mouth, but closed it again. Nothing I could say right now would make any difference.

So I just took back the newspaper.

"Okay, goin' back to Ace's," I finally said. "Homework."

Before he could say anything, I escaped out the back door.

*T*HERE WE SAT, cross-legged on the floor of Ace's bedroom, staring at my blank entry form.

"He said *no*?"

"I *told* you he'd say no!" But hollering didn't make me feel any better. And being right didn't make me feel any better either.

Ace still couldn't believe it. "But *we* gave Joe Daggett the idea!"

I shook my head. "All we told him was that it'd be swell to wear a Pups uniform. That's not the same as having a whole contest."

"Okay, so it was Joe Daggett's idea. But your pop likes Joe Daggett. He's like *this* with Joe Daggett." Ace held up two crossed fingers.

"Joe Daggett asked my pop to shine his shoes, not to be his best friend." I sighed. "Now what am I gonna do?"

"Like I said before," said Ace. "Tell your folks there's a field trip that Saturday."

"Like *I* said before, that's a dumb idea. They'd never buy that in a million years."

Ace opened his mouth to say something else, but then he frowned and cocked his head. "Hear that?"

I held still for a few seconds, listening. And then I heard it too. A *clink* at the bedroom window.

Then another one, a little louder. *CLINK.*

We went over and rolled up the window shade. Down on the sidewalk, someone was winding up to toss another pebble.

"It's Pete," grumbled Ace. "And Chuck and Charlie, and the whole sorry bunch of 'em." He slid the window up and leaned out. "What do you knuckleheads want?"

Pete sneered up at us. The rest of the fellas hovered around him like flies on a pile of rhino dung. "I shoulda figured you'd be there, Spirakis. You're just the two losers I wanna see." Pete reached into the pocket of his bomber jacket and pulled out a scrap of paper. "My entry form is all filled out," he called, waving it in the air. "If you know what's good for you, you won't even bother. Or I'll crush you both like the slimy little snails you are, and I don't mean on the ball field either."

The other fellas snorted and nodded. They're not bad eggs, on their own. But for some reason, whenever Pete's around, they all turn into drooling idiots. Like now.

"Is that what you came here for?" hollered Ace. "Well, you're wasting your time. 'Cause not only are we gonna enter, but we're gonna whip your knuckleheaded noggin all the way to Lake Michigan!"

I couldn't top that, so I didn't say anything.

Pete kept going. "Spirakis, what makes you think you'd catch a single fly ball in that contest? Even without Tank breathing down your neck, you're the saddest excuse for an outfielder I ever saw. Heck, even Ace here would do better'n you. But then of course, Ace would stink it up at the plate. The only reason he ever gets on base is because his strike zone is so small."

The drooling idiots snorted and snickered again.

Now I was mad. Mostly because Pete was saying stuff like that in front of everyone.

But also because a lot of what he said was true.

"You gotta lot of nerve comin' around here making threats, Pete!" I hollered. And then, almost before I realized what my own mouth was doing, I hollered something else at him, but this time I hollered it in Greek.

Pete stopped in midbrag. It was hard to tell for sure, because the streetlamps weren't very bright, but I could've sworn his face went pale.

And then he said something back to me, in Greek. It was just one word, but trust me when I say I can't write it down, in any language.

Everyone else stood there, staring. First at me, and then at Pete, and then at me again. But I wasn't going to explain what I'd said, and I dang well knew Pete wouldn't either.

"Come on, fellas," he muttered, glaring at me out of the corner of his eye. "We got better things to do." And they all slunk off into the night like the weasels they were.

Ace was staring at me too. Finally he said, "Well? What did you tell him?"

I slid the window closed. "Nothin'. I called him a name."

And before Ace could ask me any more questions, I changed the subject. "That knucklehead probably forged his ma's signature."

Ace cocked an eyebrow at me. "Ya think so?"

I shrugged. "It's just that one time he told me that's what he does."

Ace stared at me, and I could practically see the gears turning inside his thick noggin. "You don't suppose . . ."

"Forget it," I said. "I'm not stooping to Pete's level."

He didn't say anything. For someone with a motor-mouth, he could be even more annoying when he was quiet.

"What good would a fake signature do, anyway?" I said. "It won't spring me from work next Saturday."

Ace bit off a hangnail and spat it out. "Why can't your

uncle work for you one day? He can't claim to go to school on Saturdays, can he?"

I shook my head. "He won't set foot in that shop. I think if he ever does, he'll know he's doomed."

Ace inspected his fingernails. "In that case, I got two words for you: Field. Trip."

"I told you already, they'd never buy it." Then it hit me. "Joe Daggett!"

"What about him?"

"Remember what he said that day we met him? He said his door is always open."

"Yeah, so?"

"So what if, tomorrow after school, we go down to the Ol' Orchard to visit Joe Daggett? I can remind him how I work in my pop's shop on Saturdays, and maybe he'll let me try out on Friday after school, or Saturday after we close up shop. And then Pop will sign the permission slip too."

"It's worth a try," said Ace. "But what makes you think Joe Daggett would bend the rules just for you?"

"Don't you remember?" I held up two crossed fingers. "Me and Joe Daggett, we're like *this*."

CHAPTER

14

$\mathcal{T}$HE NEXT DAY AFTER SCHOOL, me and Ace took the same route as we had the day before, avoiding the zoo and the ball field. We had more important things to do today than play Scramble.

"Where are we going?" said Ace when I kept going past the streetcar stop. "I thought you wanted to go to the Orchard to see Joe Daggett."

"The streetcar will take too long," I said. "Follow me."

A few minutes later we banged through my front door.

"It's me, Ma!" I yelled toward the kitchen. I took the stairs two at a time, with Ace following.

At the top of the stairs, the bathroom door was shut. On the other side, someone was whistling "In the Mood."

I knocked. "Uncle Spiro?"

The whistling stopped. The door opened a few inches, and Spiro poked his head out through a cloud of steam. "Hiya, squirts," he said, rubbing his wet hair with a towel. "What's all the hubbub?"

"We need a ride," I said. "Now."

"Is that so," said Uncle Spiro. "Got a hot date?" He winked.

"Gotta get to Orchard Field," said Ace.

Spiro stopped rubbing his head. "Orchard Field? There's no game today, is there?"

"We gotta talk to someone in the front office."

Spiro cocked an eyebrow. "So take the streetcar."

"It'll take too long," I told him. "The office might close before we get there. Please?"

Ace piped up. "There's this contest," he said. "We're gonna show that Pete a thing or two, ain't that right, Nick?" He shadowboxed at the puffs of steam.

Spiro squinted at us. "Pete Costas, from over on Cherry Street?"

Ace and I both nodded.

Spiro disappeared behind the bathroom door for a second, and then reappeared in his bathrobe. "Sorry, kiddies," he said as he lathered his face at the mirror. "I'm sure Pete deserves whatever you want to do to him, but I can't help you right now. I gotta get to school." He scraped the razor across his cheek.

I was ready for this. It was a card I didn't really want to play, but I didn't have much choice. "You don't want me to tell Pop that you don't actually *go* to school, do you?"

Spiro's mouth dropped open.

"We'll be waiting in the car." We bolted downstairs before he could say anything.

"Nicky?" called Ma from the kitchen. "You want a snack?"

"Not now, Ma. Uncle Spiro's gonna take us downtown." I paced the hallway.

"A snack sounds good," said Ace.

"Later!"

A minute later, Spiro came rattling down the stairs, buttoning his shirt. "Let's go. Back door." He swept past us, trailing the scents of Barbasol and licorice gum.

We hustled after him, through the kitchen and out the back door, leaving Ma to call after us. "Why you go out with wet hair, Spiro? You'll get sick! Did you take a bath? You took a bath yesterday!"

Once we were in the car and rolling down the alley, Spiro started. "Okay, you little blackmailers. What makes you think I'm not going to night school?"

"We have our waaays, seeee," snarled Ace from the back seat. He'd been listening to too many detective dramas on the radio.

"We saw you last night, okay?" I'd already blindsided

my uncle once. The least I could do was to be honest now. "You said you were going to school, but we saw you driving in the other direction."

"Oh," said Spiro, but he didn't bother putting up a fight. "Just don't say anything to your pop, will ya? He already busts my chops, and I don't need any more grief." He chomped on his gum.

I shrugged. "Where *do* you go, anyway? I won't tell."

"Never you mind," said Uncle Spiro, rubbing my crew cut. "It's nothing shifty or anything. I'd just rather not say right now."

"Fine by me," I said.

Spiro slowed to a stop at the entrance to the ballpark. Just like Chuck had said, work crews were all over the place, hammering and sanding and painting. Sure enough, Joe Daggett was really going to Shake Things Up.

"How long do you need?" said Uncle Spiro.

"Fifteen minutes?" I told him, and Ace nodded.

"Tell you what," said Spiro, checking his watch. "I'll run a quick errand and meet you back here in twenty. Deal?"

"Deal." We slid out onto the sidewalk and waved.

"How did you know it would work?" said Ace as we watched the Nash drive away.

Finally, I could breathe again. "I didn't."

CHAPTER

15

TWENTY MINUTES LATER we were back out on the sidewalk. The Nash was already waiting at the curb, so we climbed in.

"Well?" said Uncle Spiro brightly. "Mission accomplished?"

"No." I slammed the car door, hard.

"Why not?" said Spiro.

"Joe Daggett was out," said Ace as he slid into the back seat. "He's in Sheboygan for the Pups' road trip. How do ya like that?"

Spiro's eyebrows shot up. "Joe Daggett? You came to see the new head honcho of the Mudpuppies?"

"Oh yeah, we're like *this* with Joe Daggett," said Ace, waving his crossed fingers in the air. "But his scary secretary doesn't know that. So we said to that secretary, we said, 'Tell Joe Daggett that his buddies Ace and Nick want a word with him.' We left our calling card, if you know what I mean."

"No," said Spiro, looking at Ace in the rearview mirror. "What *do* you mean?"

"He means that the scary secretary told us to write our names and phone numbers on a card," I told him.

"Oh," said Spiro. "What kind of contest is it, anyway?"

I didn't want to say too much. Uncle Spiro was being a good sport right now, but he was still a grown-up. If push came to shove, he'd have to side with Ma and Pop. I think that's a rule.

So of course Ace said, "The winner gets to be Mudpuppy for a Day! There's a field skills contest, but it's next Saturday and Nick has to work."

Ace and his big mouth.

"So that's why you tried asking your pop for the day off," said Spiro as we pulled away from the curb. "At supper last night."

"He didn't even hear me," I muttered. "And then when I asked him again, he said no."

Uncle Spiro shook his head and chomped his gum. "Sorry about that, kid. I wish I could help, but my Saturdays are booked solid."

"It's all right," I said, but I didn't sound very convincing.

We stopped at a red light, and Spiro glanced over at me. "Your pop means well, you know. He's just kind of tone deaf when it comes to kids. He didn't have much of a childhood himself."

"What do you mean?"

The light changed to green, and Spiro rolled forward. "You've heard about how *his* pop came from Greece first, and then sent for the rest of the family?"

"A million times," I said.

"Well," said Spiro, "did he ever tell you that it took your grandfather ten years to save up enough money to send for them? That whole time, your pop and grandmother were still in Greece, in that little village with no running water. Going hungry. I don't think George will ever get over the fear of having nothing. That's why he works so hard."

"Wow," was all I could say.

"Anyway, I know that doesn't help you with your problem," said Spiro. "I'd put in a word for you, but you know what that's worth."

"I know," I said. "Anyhow, that's why we went to see Joe Daggett. He knows I work on Saturdays. I figured I'd ask him if I could try out another time. But he wasn't there, so I left him a note, with my name and telephone number, and the scary secretary said she'd give it to him. She said he might get back to his office tonight. Maybe he'll call."

"Maybe he will," said Spiro cheerfully. "Things usually

have a way of working out. How about we get some frozen custard? What's your favorite, Happy's or Roger's?"

"I'm not a little kid anymore," I told him. "I don't need custard to help me feel better."

"I do," said Ace from the back seat. "Let's go to Roger's." Good ol' Ace.

"Happy's custard is better," I said.

"Is that so?" said Spiro. "I suppose there's one way to find out. Who's game for a taste test?"

I snorted. "Ma will kill us for snacking so close to suppertime."

Spiro grinned. "So, we won't tell her."

Maybe I was wrong about whose side my uncle was on, after all.

Then I looked at him sideways. "Don't you have to get to school?"

He winked at me and chomped his gum. "School? What school?"

Half an hour later we were stuffed full of custard and still arguing about whose was better.

"Happy's is creamier," I said. "You gotta admit."

"Yeah, but Roger's is more chocolatey," said Ace.

"That's all well and good," said Spiro. "But wait'll you try South Side Lenny's."

"Thanks for the ride," I said as we rolled into the alley behind the house. "And for the custard."

"It's okay, squirt," he said. "Now that I, uh, missed my first class, might as well stay for supper."

"Yikes! Supper!" said Ace as he slid out of the car. "See ya later!" He vaulted over the hedge that separated our backyards, and disappeared through a cloud of bedsheets that were hanging out to dry.

Spiro stared after him. "For a little guy, he sure can pack it away."

"That's Ace for ya."

"Nicky!" said Ma as I opened the back door. "Supper, it's ready, come and wash up, your father is hungry! Spiro! Supper!" She was carving a chicken, and Pop was already sitting at the table, smoothing his napkin onto his lap.

"Nicky!" He smiled and wiggled his eyebrows, which made me think of jumping black caterpillars. Then Pop pulled something out of his shirtfront pocket and waved it at me.

It was Joe Daggett's business card.

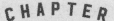

*H*IYA, POP," I said. "What's up?"

"Guess who telephoned me?" announced Pop, still waving the card. "Mister Joe Daggett!"

I stood there with my mouth hanging open, like a dope. "He did? When?"

"A few minutes ago," said Pop. "Long distance, all the way from Sheboygan!"

"How about that, squirt?" said Spiro as we soaped up at the sink. "His scary secretary must have given him the message."

Ma set a platter on the table. "Sit! Eat!"

"I gotta eat quick, Athena," said Spiro, pulling up a chair. "I'm already late for school." He shot me a warning look, but my lips were sealed. A favor for a favor.

Pop slammed his fork onto the table and glared at his brother, but didn't say a word.

Spiro sat down and helped himself to a chicken leg. "You've outdone yourself again, Athena. Where are you buying your meat nowadays? Over at the A&P?"

Ma gasped as if he'd said a swear word. "The A&P? I buy meat only from Mister Mancini's on the Frederick Street. He is the best butcher in town."

"Ya don't say." Spiro nodded as if he was actually interested. But I knew he was just trying to change the subject, as usual.

"Pop," I said, trying to sound casual. "What did Joe Daggett want?"

But Pop just said, "You know why that butcher is the best? Because he works hard, that's why." He dragged his stare away from Spiro and landed it on me. "I had a very nice talk with Mister Daggett," he said, his face relaxing. "He wanted to tell me about the contest for the boys. The one in the newspaper. He told me anyone could win the contest. He said *you* could win, maybe. And I told him, 'My Nikko can do anything, if he tries!'"

Pop is always saying stuff like that. I bet he'd say it even if you told him that if I flapped my arms really hard, I could fly.

"And you know what Mister Daggett said to me?" Pop lifted his chin and shook his fork. "He said to me, 'George, you are a very smart man.'"

Uncle Spiro heaped a pile of potatoes onto his plate. "This Daggett fella sounds like quite a salesman, if you ask me."

Pop scooped some peas. "He is not a salesman, if you must know. He is the big boss of the Mudpuppies. He said he hopes to see you at the Orchard Field on next Saturday morning, Nicky."

Was I hearing this right? Had Joe Daggett actually gone to bat for me? I tore into a chicken wing. I was pretty hungry after all.

"How about that, squirt?" said Spiro. "What d'ya say, George? Give the kid the day off."

Pop dabbed his mouth with his napkin. "Of course, I remind Mister Daggett that you work on Saturdays. He said he wishes you could try out another time, but that wouldn't be fair to the other boys. I tell him that you don't want special treatment, anyway."

"You told him *that*?" I groaned through a mouthful of chicken.

Pop nodded and helped himself to the potatoes. "I tell Mister Daggett that you are a smart boy. You know that baseball is fun to play, but work must always come before play. You know that you have responsibilities. Mister Daggett is a businessman. I know he must understand this too."

"For crying out loud, George." Uncle Spiro tossed his napkin onto the table and scraped his chair backward. "I gotta get to school."

And just like that, he was out the back door.

"He didn't eat much," declared Ma, sighing. "I don't think he liked it."

And there I sat, left to fend for myself. It was time to face facts: Joe Daggett had gone to bat for me, but he struck out swinging.

"That's okay, Pop," I said with my most casual voice. If I had to fend for myself, then I'd fend as hard as I could. "I like baseball and all, but contests aren't for me." I speared a forkful of potato, but I couldn't eat it, and it wasn't only because of all that custard. But then my mouth took on a life of its own and said, all by itself, "And anyhow, didn't I tell ya? There's a big school field trip next Saturday." I gulped. What was I doing? "To the state capitol." I shoved the potato into my mouth to keep it from saying any more stupid stuff.

Ma gave me a suspicious look. "All the way to Madison?"

"I never hear of the school trips on a Saturday," said Pop, scratching his head.

I took a few gulps of milk, to buy some time to think. There was no going back now. "Yeah, well, it's a long way, that's right, but my teacher, she said we got such great scores on our civics test that she's gonna take us as a reward, and if we go on a Saturday we won't miss regular school." I shoved another hunk of potato into my mouth.

They both sat there, rolling the idea around in their heads. Then Ma's face relaxed. She reached across the table and pinched my cheek. "You are a lucky boy, to have such a good teacher who works so hard to help you learn."

"Your mama is right," said Pop. "The work is important, but the school? That is the *most* important." He beamed at me. "Don't you worry about the shop. You just go and learn." He stabbed another piece of chicken and pulled it onto his plate.

And that's what happens when you're left to fend for yourself, and when you let your mouth talk without first checking in with your brain.

But you know what? I thought my mouth was pretty smart just then.

I ate a couple more bites of dinner and asked to be excused.

"Only one helping?" Ma said. "Are you getting sick?"

"I'm fine, Ma, thanks."

And before they could ask me any more questions, I ran upstairs to practice forging my pop's signature.

CHAPTER

17

*B*Y THE NEXT DAY, word of the contest was out. Everybody and his brother was staking out their practice territory.

Me and Ace headed to the zoo, and claimed Mountain Goat Mountain for ourselves. The goats were skittish, so they steered clear. Lucky for us, there weren't many people around, since the zoo wasn't officially open yet. Anyhow, if anyone saw us up on the rocks, we'd be through the fence and gone before they had time to find a zookeeper.

We decided to take turns. I started on the flats, and Ace climbed up with the baseball (to toss me high fly balls) and a pair of binoculars (to act as lookout). If Pete or one of his toadies was sneaking around to spy on us, Ace would see them coming.

Meanwhile, Pete set up his base of operations near the bear dens, on the other side of the zoo. (Ace's binoculars came in handy for that, too. There's nothing wrong with spying if *you're* the ones doing it.) Between us sat the Scramble field: neutral territory. If the whole team wasn't playing there, no one was playing there.

"What's up with Pete?" I asked after we'd tossed the ball a few times.

Ace checked with the binoculars. "I can't see him anymore. Hang on." He climbed all the way to the top of the rocks, sending a couple of mountain goats scrambling down the other side. He settled himself and checked the binoculars again. "There he is. He's showing off to Chuck and Charlie. Calling his shot like he's Babe Ruth. What a knucklehead!"

"What ya doing?" I heard this other voice behind me. A sickly, singsongy, girl voice.

I turned in the middle of winding up, and there she was, on the other side of the fence: that dark-haired girl with the bubblegum and saddle shoes. Penny, I think she said.

"What's it look like we're doing?" I answered. It was supposed to sound tough, but it came out kind of squeaky instead.

She tilted her head and blew a bubble. "Everybody's playing baseball," she said. "It's because of that contest next week, huh?"

I nodded and ignored her at the same time. Why was this girl hanging around? I needed to practice.

"Want some help?"

I looked up. "Huh?"

"With the fly balls," she said. "Want me to throw you some?"

So she could humiliate me all over again? "No thanks," I said. "Ace and me, we're practicing."

She stood there and blew another bubble. "It looks like Ace is busy with his binoculars. I don't have a mitt, though. And I don't think I can use yours."

Darn right she couldn't use mine.

Then I figured, if I let her try and catch one or two, maybe she'd leave us alone. I sighed really loud, to give her the hint, and then I hollered for Ace to toss down his mitt.

"Is he supposed to be up there?" said the new girl, pushing back her mess of hair.

"Sure," I said, squeezing out through the opening in the fence. "He lives there. His mother's a mountain goat." I handed her Ace's glove, but she just stood there staring at it, like she didn't know what it was for.

"It goes on your left hand," I said. "So you can throw with your right." Gee whiz. Girls.

She pulled on the mitt, looking clumsy. Probably it was the first time she'd ever used a baseball mitt. Or maybe it was the thought of Ace cooties (and who could blame her?).

I tossed her a few easy lobs, and she dropped the ball every time. She even threw the ball like a girl. Nothing like the rocket she'd thrown the other day. Which proves that the other day was a fluke.

"Never mind," she said after a couple minutes, awfully cheerful for someone who'd just looked ridiculous. "Thanks anyway."

And just like that, she handed back the mitt and marched off, with her cloud of hair flying and her socks bunched down around the tops of her saddle shoes.

I watched her leave. To make sure she wasn't coming back, that's all.

"What did Penny want?" called Ace from up high.

"No idea."

"Maybe you shoulda recruited her as a spy," he said as he scanned the zoo with his binoculars. "We could send her over to bug Pete and report back to us."

I snorted at him, but then I stopped. He didn't know it, but Ace might've hit the nail on the head. Why would a girl turn up out of nowhere and ask to play catch? Maybe Penny was already a spy. For Pete.

"Keep an eye out for that girl," I called up to Ace. "I don't trust her."

Ace laughed. "You're nuts. She's just a goofy girl, that's all. What does she care about baseball and stuff?"

Good question. "It's just weird, that's all. I'd never seen

her before the other day, and now she's everywhere. Maybe Pete's paying her or something."

Ace laughed again. "Not a chance. Pete's a tightwad. He won't ever chip in when we need to buy a new ball. Besides, you heard what she said the other day about the Fig Newtons. I don't think she's in a hurry to be friends with Pete." He did a sweep with the binoculars, stopped all of a sudden, yelped, and scrambled down the mountain. "Zookeeper coming!" He slipped through the fence and kept going toward the ball field.

I ran after him, wondering if the zookeeper had been tipped off by a tall, black-haired girl blowing bubbles.

CHAPTER 18

*S*ATURDAY. One week until the contest.

At the shop, when I wasn't shining shoes or sweeping floors, I did as many extra chores as I could, to make up for missing next Saturday.

Ace steered clear all day. He said he didn't want to distract me, but I think he just didn't want Pop to grill him about next week's "field trip." Ace is the kind of guy who cracks under pressure, and we both know it.

On Sunday during church I practiced in my head. I closed my eyes and imagined the ball sailing into my glove like a pin to a magnet. But Ma nudged me and whispered something about falling asleep in church, which I wasn't doing at all. But I could see how it might look that way to somebody else, I guess.

There sat Pete, across the aisle, between his ma (who doesn't like me, for some reason) and his big sister Sophie (who wears too much perfume and lipstick). He kept giving me the stink-eye, which I hope is a sin if you do it in church. He even had the nerve to bring a baseball. He kept sneaking it out of his jacket pocket, just so I could catch a glimpse of it.

Even in church, Pete's a show-off.

I started daydreaming about Pete dropping that baseball of his. I imagined it rolling up the aisle to the front of the church, bumping against the icon screen and sitting there, right at the feet of the priest, who'd pick it up, hitch up his robes, and hurl it all the way to the back pews. And then he'd banish Pete from church, and baseball, forever.

It was a swell daydream.

This time maybe I did doze off after all, because I jumped when Ma nudged me again. And then *she* gave me the stink-eye, which probably isn't a sin if your mother does it, even in church.

When the service was done and everyone was shuffling out, I hung back so I wouldn't have to bump into Pete. But somehow I bumped into his sister instead, which was worse.

"Hello there, Nicky," she said to me, all sugary sweet. She had a smear of lipstick on her teeth.

"Hey, Sophie." I needed to get out of there. I'd already

spent two hours in church. Not even God could expect me to hang around longer than that, especially talking to Pete's smelly big sister.

But Sophie tugged at my arm. "Where's that uncle of yours? How come I haven't seen him in church lately?"

I happened to know that Uncle Spiro was a shameless heathen who avoided church religiously. Probably because it aggravated the heck out of Pop. But all I said to Sophie was, "Why don't you ask him yourself sometime?" I pulled away from her greedy grip, trying not to shudder too much, since I was still in church.

"I would, if I ever saw him around, silly!" She kept smiling, but her extra-red lips looked a little stiff. "Tell him hello, won't you? Give him *filaki* for me!" And then she actually bent down and tried to kiss my cheek. Can you believe the nerve? Just because she wears lipstick and stockings and thinks she's all grown up. No girl who's not my mother is going to kiss me. I turned tail and got out of there, fast.

Ma and Pop were already at the car. I climbed into the back seat, kicking aside the empty gum wrappers, cigarette packs, and custard spoons that littered the floor. Uncle Spiro was not the neatest guy in the world.

"I see you talking to Sophia Costas in church," said Ma from the front seat.

"Not exactly." I shifted on the seat. The gum wrappers crinkled under me. "*She* was talking to *me*."

"You be nice to Sophia," said Ma, as if I'd just threat-ened to call the lipstick police or something. "Her mother is a very important woman at the church, you know. In charge of the Ladies' Guild."

Ma said "in charge of the Ladies' Guild" the way other people might say "the Queen of England." The annual church festival was coming up soon, and Ma had been try-ing for months to get her *koulouria* accepted for the bake sale. Apparently the only thing standing in the way was Mrs. Costas. It's an undisputed fact that Ma's *koulouria* are the best cookies in the entire parish, so of course I wondered if Ma wasn't getting anywhere with the Queen of England because of the fact that Her Majesty did not like me. For some reason.

Pop made a grumbling noise. "Why Sophia Costas was talking to Nicky? It's not ladylike, for the girl to approach the boy. And the rouge all over her face. She try too hard."

"What else she should do?" said Ma. "Almost twenty years old and not married yet. What she's waiting for?"

Apparently, she was waiting for Uncle Spiro.

"Her father must tell her who she will marry," said Pop. "What *he* is waiting for?" He swerved the Nash around a pothole.

Ma made a *tsk*ing noise. "This is not the old country!" she said. "The young people, they want to make their own life. The arranged marriage is not for them."

"Why not?" hollered Pop. "It was good enough for us! Don't we have a good life? Aren't we happy?"

"Sure we are happy!" Ma hollered back. "What does Sophia Costas know about making a good life with a good man? Nothing." She crossed her arms, as if everything was settled and Sophie Costas was doomed. Which maybe she was, if she kept her sights trained on Uncle Spiro. I happened to know that he was just as terrified of her as I was.

Ma turned toward the back seat. "Nicky," she said, her voice melting. "Why not ask Taki Costas to come play at the house sometime? You go to school together, *neh*? You should be friends."

"Pete?" I jolted back in the seat as if we'd just hit another pothole.

I should explain. In Greek, Pete's name is Panagiotakis. Taki, for short. Pete hates that nickname (and who can blame him, but better him than me). One time, in second grade, he actually punched a kid for calling him Taki to his face.

"I don't think that's a good idea, Ma."

"Why not?" she said. "His mother is a very important woman at the church, you know."

"I know," I muttered. "She's the Queen of England."

93

CHAPTER

19

I MAY HAVE MENTIONED already that I'm not very good at writing in Greek, what with only twenty-four letters at my disposal. To be perfectly honest, I'm not all that great when all twenty-six letters are available either.

I don't exactly stink at writing. Not the way I stink at fielding, anyway. Let's just say that if I could choose one skill at which the cards are stacked sky high against me (besides catching fly balls) it would be writing an essay. But once you've decided to forge your pop's signature (in order to show up that bigmouthed, knuckleheaded Pete), you do what you gotta do.

So there we sat on Monday after supper, me and Ace, on the floor of his bedroom, surrounded by pencils, erasers, and a zillion crumpled sheets of composition paper. Because not only is it hard to write a decent essay (even with all twenty-six letters of the alphabet), it's even harder when you have to do it in a hundred words or less. Try it sometime.

"Are you sure it didn't say a hundred words or *more*?" said Ace.

"A hundred words or *less*," I told him. "I double checked."

"It's impossible to explain how swell I am in only a hundred words," he said. "That's barely half a page. I'm already on page three, and I'm just gettin' started."

"I know," I said. "I'm having the same problem."

He chewed his pencil for a while. "That does it," he said finally. "I'm just makin' a list."

I shook my head. "That's not an essay. You don't want to get disqualified on a technicality, do you?"

"Why isn't it an essay?"

"Because an essay has . . . I dunno . . . sentences and stuff."

Ace stared at the sheet of paper in his hand. Then he sighed, crumpled it up, and started over.

After about eighty years (okay, maybe twenty minutes) of pure torture, I put down my pencil and cleared my throat. "How does this sound?"

> *"If I could be MUDPUPPY FOR A DAY, I'd never want anything else in my whole life. I would be best because I need this job. My Pop started a new life*

when he was 12 yrs old. Now I'm 12 years old and I
want to start my own new life. My Pop says I work
hard, and so I would work hard for the Mudpupies.
I would be the best batboy. I hope you give me a
chance to show you how I would be the best. I dont
think a bat boy needs to catch fly balls. That would
not be fare to the feilders. Besides, it is there job.
Signed, Nick Spirakis."

"That's swell," said Ace, and I could tell he was
impressed. "How many words?"

I counted. "Dang. A hundred and sixteen."

"Does your name count?"

"I dunno. The rules don't say."

Ace chewed his pencil, thinking. "Don't they know it's
you already? I mean, your name will be on the entry form,
right?"

He was right. I erased "Signed, Nick Spirakis." "A hundred and thirteen words."

He chewed his pencil some more. He tapped the page.
"You say 'I would be the best' in a bunch of different places,"
he said. "Cross one out."

I crossed out and counted. "A hundred and eight."

"Isn't that close enough?" said Ace.

"I don't think so."

He studied my paper again. After a minute he told me,

"You say 'I work hard' in a bunch of places too. Get rid of one."

"But I *do* work hard. I really think they ought to know that."

Ace shrugged. "Just trying to help."

I scowled for a minute and stared at my essay. Then I crossed out some more words, and counted.

"Ha!" I said. "Ninety-nine. Let's hear yours."

But he pulled his paper to his chest. "No."

"Why not?"

His ears went red. "It stinks. I'm not done. I got a long way to go." Now his face was going red too. "I need a break. Wanna go toss the ball around?"

And so we scooped up all the crumpled paper, chucked it into the wastebasket, grabbed our mitts, and headed outside.

You might be wondering why me and Ace bothered to help each other, since only one person could be Mudpuppy for a Day.

First of all, we've been best friends since kindergarten, and that's what best friends do. I'm pretty sure that's a rule (and if it's not, it should be).

Second, winning is more fun if you beat someone who's top-notch. For example, I could beat my ma in a footrace, but it wouldn't be as much fun as beating my Uncle Spiro.

Third, me and Ace were united against a common enemy, and his name was Pete.

So every day that week, right after school (except on Tuesday, on account of Greek school), me and Ace headed over to Mountain Goat Mountain.

And every day, there sat Penny on the park bench, swinging her feet and watching us. I don't mean casual watching either. I mean *really* watching. Every throw, every catch. Every *missed* catch too. She never made a peep, though. She just sat there, blowing bubbles and watching.

I don't mind saying, it made me nervous. And also very suspicious. Why would a girl be so interested in a couple of fellas playing baseball, unless she was up to something? She was new in town—for all I knew, she was in cahoots with Pete. That story of hers about Pete and the bubblegum in the Fig Newtons—the more I thought about it, the more I decided it was a bunch of malarkey. No one does something like that to Pete and gets away with it. Maybe she'd made up that whole story so she could come around every day to spy on us and then report our doings to Pete.

I tried to forget about it. What could she report, anyway—that I was a lousy outfielder? Pete already knew that. And even after practicing all week, by Friday I was still a lousy outfielder.

That was a problem.

You might think it was because of that incident with the rhinoceros. But I'm not so sure it's Tank's fault. Sometimes I think I'd stink up the outfield even if Tank was replaced by a field full of bunnies. I mean, other fellas have had to climb into the rhino yard, and it hasn't stopped *them* from being able to catch the ball. (Then again, I was the only one who ever got personally escorted out by Tank, so to speak.) Anyway, for whatever reason, it happens every time: I see a fly ball coming my way, and I freeze.

So now it was Friday, the day before the contest. Me and Ace were practicing, as usual, when here comes Penny again, with her wild black hair blowing loose from her headband. But today she was carrying a beat-up leather pocketbook, and she was wearing overalls. Like she was Rosie the Riveter or something.

"Hiya, Nick," she said, plopping down on the bench just outside the fence, like she'd done almost every day that week.

"Hiya. We're kinda busy."

"Where's Ace?"

"Up there somewhere." I pointed toward the top of Mountain Goat Mountain.

Just then, a voice hollered "Incoming!" A second later, a baseball sailed over the top of the rocks. It hit its apex and hung there for a fraction of a second, like an eyeball that was looking for me. And then it found me, and came roaring down in my direction.

The one thing I did *not* need right now was an audience.

I held out my glove, but of course I missed the ball. It bounced on the ground next to me, bumped against the fence, and landed at my feet.

My face burned. Because I knew she was watching.

And then, for the first time all week, Penny piped up. I thought she was going to laugh, but she just said, "You're not reading the ball."

I turned around and gave that girl the stink-eye. "What are ya talking about? You don't *read* a baseball; you catch it."

"*You* don't do either one," she said.

This girl was driving me crazy.

"We're kinda busy," I told her again.

She did not take the hint. In fact, she said, "I was wondering if I could play today." She patted the hunk of beat-up leather on her lap, which was not a pocketbook after all. It was a baseball glove.

"What's that, your brother's old mitt?" I said.

Without batting an eye, she said, "My sister's." Deadpan humor, that's what Penny had.

Why did she keep coming around here? Maybe I'd been right about her all along, and she really was a spy for Pete. I opened my mouth to chase her away for good.

"Hiya, Penny!" It was Ace, up on the mountain. He climbed down while the mountain goats peeked at him from behind the rocks. "Hey, you brought a glove? Swell! You wanna help us practice?"

What was he doing? I wanted to chuck something at him. We'd given her a chance already, when we'd let her borrow Ace's glove, and she'd stunk it up pretty bad.

"Why do you wanna play ball, anyway?" I said.

"Shouldn't you be playing dolls, or wearing pink stuff, or doing whatever girls do after school?"

She didn't take the bait. "That stuff's boring," she said. "I like to be outside. And I like you two guys okay. All those other boys are knuckleheads."

I scuffed the ground with my foot. Maybe I'd been too hard on her.

"Yeah, okay, sure," I said. "You can chase after the ones that get away."

So I showed her where to squeeze in through a gap in the fence, and promised her that the mountain goats wouldn't bother her, and stationed her on the far side of the rocks.

She just better not be spying for Pete.

CHAPTER 21

I TOLD ACE TO COME DOWN off the rocks and pitch to me, because I needed some batting practice (and also a break from being embarrassed in front of a girl with my horrible fielding). I hit a few good ones too, and I have to admit: Penny did a pretty good job chasing them down. She even managed to catch a screaming line drive. She did way better than the day she'd borrowed Ace's glove. It helps to have a glove you're used to, I suppose.

So as I was saying, Ace was pitching to me. But I was a little distracted, because something about Penny was bugging me. At first I thought it was the whole idea of playing with a girl, but that wasn't it (especially because I practically forgot she was a girl, in those overalls). Then I thought maybe it was how good she was, for a girl. But that wasn't it either. I couldn't quite put my finger on it, though.

Then I figured it out, when I hit the next pitch and she reached out and grabbed it without batting an eye.

"You're a lefty!"

She stood there looking at me with her head to one side, like everyone in the world knew that except me.

"That's why you stunk it up with Ace's glove," I said. "Why didn't you say something?"

She tossed the ball back to Ace and blew a bubble. "Would you have let me play that day if I had?"

Probably not.

I was still thinking about that on the next pitch, so I swung under the ball, and I popped it up.

What happened next was a thing of beauty.

Penny froze for a second, her face lifted toward the sky. Then she took a few steps back. She raised her arms and took a few steps forward. A second later, the ball fell into her glove like an egg dropping into a nest.

Penny showed me the ball, grinning and chomping her gum.

"Nice catch!" said Ace. "Where'd you learn to play like that?"

"I told you," said Penny, tossing Ace the ball. "From my sister. You know, Nick, if you wanted, I could give you a few pointers. I've been watching you all week. It's just a matter of reading the ball."

I opened my mouth to tell her off. She had a lot of nerve. A girl, teaching a fella how to play ball?

Of course, I really needed to win this contest. And I needed all the help I could get. And she *was* really good.

But come on. A *girl*, who apparently learned everything she knew from *another* girl?

I looked her right in the eye and said, "Yeah, sure, I guess."

So I took the outfield while Ace pitched and Penny hit pop-ups, one after another. She explained what she meant about reading the ball.

"Don't chase it right away," she said. "Hold still for a second and watch it jump off the bat. That way, you'll see where the ball is going, and you'll know which direction— and how fast—to run."

And sure enough: After a few tries, I actually caught a pop fly.

All this made me think maybe I'd misjudged Penny. Maybe she wasn't a spy for Pete after all.

On the next pitch, Penny really got under the ball. She hit it a mile into the air.

We all stood there craning our necks, waiting to see where the ball was gonna come down. A second later, it came whistling down just outside the tall fence that surrounded

Mountain Goat Mountain. It hit the asphalt path, bounced over another fence, and landed smack in the yard of the animal next store.

Tank's yard.

"I'll get it!" hollered Ace, and he headed toward the gap in the mountain goat fence.

"It's getting dark," I told him. "Leave it till tomorrow."

We'd gone into Tank's yard a million times before, of course, but we weren't idiots. We had rules. Rule Number One: Never go over the fence unless Tank is inside his little house, or at least on the far side of his yard, near the billboard. And Rule Number Two: *Never* go over Tank's fence at dusk. Because (2a) it's hard to see the ball against all that dry grass and straw when the daylight is fading, and (2b) Tank knows that dusk means "almost dinnertime" and he tends to get feisty.

But right now, Ace wasn't listening to me. He squeezed out through the gap in the fence around Mountain Goat Mountain.

"You're not actually going into that place where that rhino is," said Penny. "Are you?"

"I done it a million times!" said Ace. If I didn't know better, I'd say he was showing off for Penny.

"But the rhinoceros is *right there*," said Penny.

She was right. Tank was so close, you could've sprayed him with an energetic sneeze.

But Ace just said, "That ain't nothin'," and before common sense got the better of him, he scurried to Tank's fence and vaulted over, right next to the sign with Tank's vital statistics.

And there stood all 2,580 pounds of Tank, twitching his tiny little ears.

Ace was so busy showing off that he hadn't stopped to locate the ball before he hopped the fence. Now he scrambled around for a second or two, trying to find it. He finally grabbed it, but by then Tank was thundering toward him like a bowling ball on a 7–10 split.

Lucky for Ace, he's small and fast and hard to catch. He outran Tank by inches, and hurled himself up and over the fence just in time. But his foot got caught in the chain link or something, because instead of coming down feet first, he flipped over and landed almost on his head.

Tank grunted and went back to chewing the clover.

There sat Ace, all in a heap. He untangled his feet and blinked up at me and Penny like he was surprised to see us. Then he saw the ball in his hand.

"Hey, look!" he said.

And then he fainted. Which is even more embarrassing than missing a fly ball in front of a girl.

And that's how Ace broke his arm, the day before the contest.

CHAPTER 22

I'VE BEEN PUTTING THIS OFF, but it's time to admit: I'm a pretty good liar. Ma and Pop swallowed the whole story about a Saturday field trip to Madison.

I told them that there'd be a bus leaving school at ten o'clock and dropping us off again at three. (The contest would probably be finished way before then, but if I showed up at home too early, Ma would figure out we hadn't actually gone all the way to Madison. Just because she can't read English doesn't mean she was born yesterday.)

The plan was to meet Ace out front at nine o'clock, so we'd get to Orchard Field in plenty of time. We decided to avoid each other's folks as much as possible before then, so we wouldn't have to worry about keeping our stories straight, or (in Ace's case) blabbing the wrong thing.

At nine o'clock sharp, we both banged out our front doors and down our porch steps. Ace had a clean new cast on his left arm, from his wrist to his elbow. There was no way he could compete now, but there was no way he was gonna miss it either. Especially after all that time he'd spent on his essay.

"Are you sure we're supposed to leave our gear at home?" he said as we met on the sidewalk. "It feels weird not bringing my own glove and bat."

I knew how he felt, but I nodded. "You read the contest rules. 'All necessary gear will be provided.' Besides, my ma would've been suspicious if she saw me leaving the house with my gear."

"I hope they have decent gear at the contest," said Ace.

I laughed. "It's a professional baseball team. I'm pretty sure they'll have decent gear."

"I guess," said Ace. "All clear at your house?"

I gave him the thumbs-up. "Pop's already at the shop, and Ma will be baking all day."

"What about Uncle Spiro?" said Ace.

I peeked back between the houses. The Nash was gone from its usual spot in the alley. "He went somewhere early, I guess."

"Swell," said Ace. "Got your entry form and essay?" He pulled a big fat envelope out of his pocket and waved it at me.

"What the heck is that?"

He looked at it. "It's my essay."

"It's supposed to be a hundred words, not a hundred pages!"

He shrugged. "It's only seventeen pages. There was no way I could explain everything in only a hundred words. I needed five pages just to tell 'em how I broke my arm."

I busted out laughing.

Ace grinned. "I can't win with a broken arm. Might as well give them something interesting to read. Got your essay?"

"Ninety-nine words," I said, showing him my own envelope, with my essay and my forged signature inside. I stopped laughing. "I feel kind of like a snake."

Ace slapped me on the back as we started up the sidewalk. "Wait'll you get to the ballpark. One look at Pete's ugly mug and you'll forget all about it. Besides, it's just a little fib. It's not like you're robbing a bank or anything."

Ace was right. This was a special, rare occasion. A one-time-only deal.

We walked up the street toward school, in case any grown-ups were looking out the window. But once we got to Frederick Street, we caught the Number 37 streetcar heading downtown.

The streetcar ride took twenty minutes or so, which was plenty of time for me to start worrying.

It was just a little fib. One time only.

I'd never actually *lied* to my folks before—not like this, a big whopper of a fib, *and* a forged signature. Just to get out of work for a few hours on a Saturday.

But what else could I do? Was it my fault I was stuck working in Pop's shop every Saturday, while Ace and Charlie and everybody else were outside having fun?

And then there was Pete. He'd been pushing me around since kindergarten, and I was tired of it.

The more I thought about it, the more I realized that a whole bunch of people spent a whole lot of time telling me what to do. The only person *not* in charge of my life was me.

So yeah, I lied. But it was one time only, and for a good cause. Everyone would understand that once I won this contest. Right?

Of course, if I didn't win, I'd be nothing but a plain old liar.

CHAPTER

23

*A*s soon as me and Ace got off the streetcar, I could practically feel the buzzing in the air. The Pups were out of town, but it felt almost like a game day, with bunches of kids heading toward Orchard Field. The whole ballpark had been painted and scrubbed. Even the sidewalks had been swept clean. Not a gum wrapper or a cigarette butt in sight.

We got in line with all the other kids heading for the turnstiles. Once we were inside, there was another line for sign-ups. You dropped your essay into a big box (Ace's fat envelope almost got stuck in the slot), handed over your permission slip, and wrote your name on the sign-up sheet. Then you got a numbered piece of paper and a safety pin. The number on the paper matched the number next to your name on the sign-up sheet. I was number seventy-two, and Ace was seventy-three.

"Pin the number on each other's backs, fellas," said the usher in charge of the sign-ups. "Once that's done, you can head on down to the field."

"Oh boy, the field!" said Ace as I pinned his number on his back. "I never been on a real baseball field before. This is gonna be swell!"

He was right. Just walking out through the grandstand and toward the field was exciting. The sun was bright, and the sky was blue, and the grass was so green it almost hurt my eyes. The only place we'd ever sat for a Mudpuppies game was the outfield bleachers, so I'd never even been this close to home plate before. And now we were being allowed right onto the field. With a zillion other fellas, of course, but I didn't care. Nobody wanted to win this contest more than me. I'd catch every fly ball that came my way, even if I had to sprout wings to do it.

"Do you see Pete anywhere?" I asked Ace as we followed everybody down the concrete steps toward the field. "Or Chuck, or Charlie, or anyone we know?"

We both scanned the crowd on the field. "Nope," said Ace. "But you know they gotta be here somewhere."

A minute later, we were actually standing on the infield grass, and the ballpark loudspeaker squealed to life.

"Good morning, everyone!" boomed a familiar voice.

"That sounds like Joe Daggett," I said.

"There he is!" said Ace.

Sure enough, there stood Joe Daggett on the pitcher's mound. He wore a suit and tie and a Mudpuppies cap, and he was leaning on a cane. In front of him was a big fat microphone on a stand. Behind him was a bunch of fellas dressed like umpires, each one holding a clipboard. His secretary—the scary lady who'd shooed us out of his office last week—wobbled next to him in her high-heeled shoes. She didn't look too happy to be out here.

"Welcome to the First Annual Mudpuppy for a Day Batboy Contest!" Joe Daggett announced into the microphone, and everyone cheered. "Glad to see such a dandy turnout today! Are you ready to show off your batboy skills?"

Another cheer went up from the crowd.

"That's what I like to hear!" The speakers squealed again, and Joe Daggett jumped back from the microphone like he'd broken it. The secretary whispered something in his ear, and he nodded. He stepped to the microphone again, but this time not as close. "Okay, I'm gonna lay out a few ground rules and then we'll get started. But first! I have a special announcement!"

A rumble of excitement went through the crowd.

Joe Daggett waved his cane in the air. "As you all know, the winner of our contest will be chosen in a special ceremony before the next Mudpuppies home game on May twenty-ninth. That's next Saturday, just one week from today!"

Everybody cheered, including me. I was too excited about today to worry about next Saturday.

"At the end of today's competition, I'll announce the three top scores."

"Three!" said Ace, grabbing at my sleeve. "How swell is that?"

"Those top three finalists will be invited back for one final round of competition on game day."

Another cheer.

"An additional three finalists will be chosen based on your essays. If you're one of those lucky fellas, you'll get an official letter from us in the mail. That means *six* lucky fellas competing for the grand prize of Mudpuppy for a Day, in front of a full house here at the Ol' Orchard!"

More cheers.

"But wait! There's more! Another big event is coming up soon, and that's the annual Zoo Spring Opening. A parade! Brass bands! Baton twirling! Sounds like loads of fun, doesn't it? And what would be more fun than combining those two big events into one?"

If a crowd of kids could holler a question mark, that's the sound we made now.

"That's right, kids," said Joe Daggett. "Maybe only one of you can be Mudpuppy for a Day, but you're *all* invited back here on May twenty-ninth. You'll each get a free bleacher ticket!"

This time we gave a real cheer.

"*And* you're all invited to follow the Spring-Opening Caravan of Animals, all the way to Orchard Field!"

We all made that question mark noise again.

"Just imagine," said Joe Daggett. "All sorts of animals, parading from the zoo to the ballpark. Zebras! Hippos! Lions!"—the secretary lady tugged his sleeve and whispered something into his ear—"Oh, sorry, no lions. (What about monkeys, Miss Garble?) Monkeys! And all sorts of other really amazing zoo animals, right here on the field at the Ol' Orchard!"

A huge whoop went up from the crowd of kids, because let's be honest: Who wouldn't love to see monkeys at the ballpark?

Joe Daggett tapped the microphone with a finger, and everyone quieted down. "Okay, fellas, let's get this contest started! Here's how it's gonna work. You'll split up into groups, and you'll rotate through four stations." He swept his cane around behind him. The secretary hopped out of the way just in time.

A buzz moved through the crowd. Now we were getting somewhere. Ace nudged me and counted on the fingers sticking out from his cast. "Hitting, base running, fielding, and throwing."

Joe Daggett raised his free arm and counted on his fingers. "Water carrying! Base dusting! Ball mudding! And sunflower seed spitting!"

Have you ever heard the sound of hundreds of mouths dropping open? It's something like the first glub of water when you pull the plug in the bathtub.

Then all the mouths exploded in cheers and whoops and hollers.

Because let's be honest again: Any contest that involves mud and spitting is A-okay. Plus, right now, hundreds of kids all decided that this might be one contest they could actually win.

Including me.

24

*J*OE DAGGETT LIMPED OFF THE FIELD, still waving his cane in the air, and the umpires divided us into groups according to our sign-up numbers. Me and Ace were in the same group. Each station would be judged by one of the umpires.

"No wonder we didn't need to bring our gloves and bats," said Ace. "Joe Daggett had something else up his sleeve."

"Joe Daggett always has something up his sleeve," I said. And then I spotted Pete, off by himself at the edge of another group, pacing the grass and muttering to himself.

I pointed him out to Ace. "He's giving himself a pep talk."

Ace snorted. "I bet he's grumbling about how he doesn't get a chance to show off with the bat. Hey look, there's Chuck and Charlie, too." Sure enough, there they were, in

Pete's group. "I hope they swallow their sunflower seeds."

"That's not nice," I said, but I laughed, because it was pretty funny.

Our group's first skill was water carrying. You had to carry a full bucket of water from home plate to first base, and whoever had the fastest time, and the fullest bucket, was the winner. Everybody got soaked, because that bucket was heavy, and it sloshed a lot. It was hilarious. The umpire used a stopwatch to measure our times and a yardstick to measure our water levels. He wrote it all down on his clipboard, but he never told us our results. I thought I did pretty good, or at least as good as anybody else.

Next was the base-dusting station. The whole group crammed into the third-base dugout, and we took turns running out to third base with a little hand broom, brushing a pile of dirt off the base, and running back again. The umpire at this station used a stopwatch too, and checked to make sure the base was good and clean. Then he scribbled on his clipboard, but didn't tell anybody what their score was.

The ball-muddying station was set up in foul territory behind home plate. Each kid got three brand-new baseballs and a coffee can full of this special mud. You had to rub the mud into the baseballs, but not too little or too much—you couldn't leave any white spots or clumps of mud. Just like the other skills, we were judged on speed and technique.

Last came sunflower seed spitting. Three lines of tape

were laid out in right field, parallel to the foul line. You stood with your toes on the foul line, and got three tries to spit a seed as far as you could (no do-overs for wind or accidental swallowing either). Any seeds that got past the farthest line were measured for distance. Ace and me both spit a seed far enough to get measured.

When everyone finished at all the stations, we all got to sit in the grandstand and eat free ice cream.

"Boy, that was swell!" said Ace. "Did you see how I spit that seed? Wanna hear my secret technique? I just imagined I was trying to hit Pete right between the eyes."

"I heard that, you little weasel!"

"Oops."

We both turned around, and there was Pete, two rows behind us, sitting between Chuck and Charlie. His face was all red, and he was still soaked from the bucket race.

"What happened to you?" said Ace, looking Pete over. "You were supposed to carry the water in the bucket, not your pockets."

Ace never would've said that if there wasn't a row of kids between him and Pete. All Pete could do was throw his empty ice cream cup at him.

Then the loudspeaker squealed, and everyone jumped to attention.

There was Joe Daggett, on the pitcher's mound again, with a clipboard in his hand.

All of a sudden my hands got clammy and my heart started pounding. "This is it!" I whispered to Ace. I suddenly wished I hadn't eaten that ice cream so fast.

"I want to congratulate all of you for a spirited competition," said Joe Daggett into the microphone. "We sure did see some nifty batboy skills today. Give yourselves a round of applause!"

The crowd in the grandstand clapped politely. Because you know we were all waiting for something else.

Joe Daggett raised the clipboard. "I have a list here of the top three scores from today's contest. These three finalists have won the right to compete again next Saturday, along with the three essay finalists, in a special pregame contest for the grand prize of Mudpuppy for a Day!"

The crowd rumbled in anticipation.

"But don't forget, you're all invited back here that day as our honored guests. Before you leave the ballpark today, be sure to collect your free game ticket! Okay, fellas, double check the numbers pinned to your backs. If I call out your number, come on down to the field."

Hundreds of kids held their breath.

"Seventy-two," I whispered to myself over and over, just in case the words would float through the air and onto Joe Daggett's clipboard.

It did not work the first time.

Or the second time. In fact, that's when things got

even worse. That's when Joe Daggett called, "Number one hundred twenty-five!"

Two rows behind us, me and Ace heard a familiar voice.

"It's about time!" Pete got up and shoved his way to the end of his row, knocking kids over like they were dominoes. He lumbered down the steps and onto the infield, joining Joe Daggett and the first kid on the pitcher's mound.

"My ma's always telling me life isn't fair," grumbled Ace. "And guess what? She's right."

But I already knew that. I squeezed my eyes shut, so I wouldn't have to look at Pete's ugly mug, and whispered, "Seventy-two, seventy-two, seventy-two . . ."

"Seventy-two!" Ace said next to me.

"I know," I said, without opening my eyes. "Seventy-two, seventy-two—"

"*Nick!*" Ace grabbed my arm. "Joe Daggett called number *seventy-two!*"

*A*FTER IT WAS ALL OVER, me and Ace sat in the infield grandstand, waiting for everyone else to clear out. We didn't want to be on the same streetcar home with Pete— who needs to hear all that bragging?—so we decided to hang back and catch the next one.

Joe Daggett had shaken hands with all the winners, and even winked at me and said, "Hey! My shoe-shine buddy!" It was pretty swell.

"I can't believe you and Pete are both finalists," said Ace. "I mean, I knew *I* wouldn't win"—he held up his cast, which was smeared pretty good with reddish baseball mud—"but gee whiz."

"He hasn't won yet," I said. "I wonder what the final contest will be?"

"With Joe Daggett in charge, it could be anything," said Ace. "Hopping around the bases on one foot. Singing 'The Star-Spangled Banner' backward. I mean, *anything*."

Ace was right.

Finally, we were the last kids left in the ballpark, so we got up to leave. Joe Daggett was gone, and so was his scary secretary. The umpire/judging crew was clearing away the last of the gear from the field.

Outside, at the streetcar stop, there was only one kid waiting. Even at a distance, I could tell it wasn't Pete. And then I knew who it was. Because of the hair.

"Penny!" I called. "What are you doing here? The bat-boy contest was today. It was swell!"

She nodded, but didn't look at us.

"Hiya, Penny!" said Ace. "Guess what? Nick's a finalist!"

"Congratulations." She was wearing her Rosie the Riveter overalls, and her face was all red and blotchy.

"What's the matter?" I said.

She just stared down the street, and then she said in a quiet voice, "They wouldn't let me play."

"Play what?" said Ace.

But I thought I knew what she meant. "You came to do the contest? But they didn't let you? Why not?"

"Because I'm a *girl*!" And then she started bawling, right there at the streetcar stop, which really made me nervous. But I couldn't blame her either.

"Aw, gee, Penny," said Ace. "That stinks. I'm sorry you're a girl."

This did not seem to make her feel any better.

"What happened?" I said.

So Penny blew her nose and told us how she showed up this morning like everybody else, with her entry form and essay and everything, but the fella at the sign-up table wouldn't give her a number because she was a girl.

"I didn't see anything in the rules about no girls," said Ace, scratching around his cast.

"It doesn't," said Penny, "except where it says it's for *boys*." She blew her nose again.

"Well, if that don't beat all," said Ace. "That's not fair! You're just as good as any boy."

"I know!" she said. That's one thing I like about Penny. She's very modest. "And then Pete saw me, and he started laughing at me, in front of everybody. He said it served me right, for putting bubblegum in his Fig Newtons."

I should've known. No one does something like that to Pete and gets away with it. I felt like a snake for ever thinking that Penny could be a spy for Pete.

"And then he said . . . he said . . ." She scrubbed away a tear that escaped down her cheek.

"You can tell us," said Ace, who had experience with girls, because of his little sister.

Penny hiccupped. "He . . . he pointed at me and said,

really loud: 'How did that hairy monkey get in here, anyway? That's right—go back home to the zoo!' And all the other boys laughed." She smoothed down her hair, which popped right back up, and she hiccupped again. "I don't care what stupid people think, or say, usually. But today . . . after the Mudpuppies told me I didn't belong there either . . . it just got to me." She sniffed a good one.

"That stupid Pete!" I said. "What does he know, anyway?"

Ace chimed in. "He's just scared of you, that's all. Afraid of being beaten by a girl. Besides, we like your hair, don't we, Nick? It has . . . *energy*."

I had to hand it to Ace. Sometimes he knew exactly the right thing to say. Penny actually smiled a little, and I could tell she felt better.

But I was hopping mad. Getting turned away from the contest was one thing. Sure, it was stupid and unfair, but at least no one *meant* to hurt Penny's feelings. Being mean to her on purpose—that was too much. I had to win this contest, even if it was only for revenge.

Penny wiped her face with a sleeve. "The man at the sign-up table let me stay and watch. I couldn't go home. What'll I tell Josie?"

"Who's Josie?" said Ace.

"My big sister," said Penny. "She'll be so disappointed."

I remembered the other day when Penny'd told us she'd borrowed her sister's glove. Maybe that wasn't a joke after all.

"It's not your fault," I said.

"Yeah," said Ace. "Your sister will still be proud of you."

Penny gave another huge sniff. "And after I finally talked my mom into signing the permission slip. I mean, if Josie can play ball, why can't I? I put my essay in the box and everything. They're just gonna throw it away. And it was a really good essay too! Exactly a hundred words."

"Nice!" said Ace, who likes to give credit where credit is due.

The Number 37 streetcar pulled up. We climbed on and squeezed into a seat together.

"Well, this isn't right," said Ace, nudging me over. "Did Joe Daggett make that rule about no girls? We oughta give him a piece of our minds."

Penny snorted. "What makes you think he'd listen to you?"

"Are you kidding?" said Ace, giving her the ol' crossed finger sign. "We're like this with Joe Daggett. Let's go back." He reached up to pull the signal cord, but I stopped him.

"What can Joe Daggett do about it now?" I said. "Even if he wanted to change the rules, it's too late. The contest is over. The damage is done."

Ace sat back down. "It's still not right."

"I know," I told him. "We'll figure out a way to make it right. Right, Penny?"

"If you say so," she said, and she gave one more gigantic sniff.

CHAPTER 26

*T*HAT NIGHT AFTER LIGHTS OUT, I stared at my bedroom ceiling, thinking about stuff.

Poor Penny. Not allowed to enter the contest just because she was a girl. She even had a signed permission slip and everything.

And I'd turned in a forged permission slip, and now I was a finalist.

I told myself that one thing had nothing to do with the other. I mean, Penny would've been rejected even if I hadn't cheated. But somehow, I felt even more like a rat than I had before.

And here's another thing about entering a contest that you don't actually have permission to enter: Who can you tell when you win?

Of course, I wasn't an actual winner—not yet, anyway. Only a finalist. Besides, what would I miss by not telling Ma and Pop? A bunch of smeary kisses, and pinched cheeks, and stuff like *What did I tell you, Athena, Nicky is the smartest boy in the whole wide world, you make us so proud, Nicky, let me kiss you again.* I'd get pretty much the same reaction by bringing home a decent grade on a geography quiz. Or putting my shoes on the right feet.

Maybe I could talk them into going to the Mudpuppies game next Saturday, and once they saw me down on the field with only five other kids, they'd understand what a big deal it was, and they'd forgive me.

Who was I kidding? Pop would be at the shop on Saturday, like always, and Ma would be at home, cooking or ironing or hanging out the wash, like always. That was the problem: they didn't know how to have fun.

But what's life without a little fun?

And where's the fun in winning if you can't brag about it, even a little?

Of course, Pete wouldn't have any trouble bragging. I would need to keep him away from Ma and Pop at church the next morning. Not that he'd brag about *me.* But you never know what he's gonna do, and he doesn't even care if he's at church. In fact, the last time Pete tried to punch me was on the steps of the church.

This was way back, at the end of second grade.

Everybody was heading outside after church one Sunday, and I spotted Pete on the sidewalk. We'd just started playing ball at the zoo that spring, and I wanted to tell him how I'd thought up the perfect name for our game. (You have plenty of time to think about stuff like that when you're sitting in church for two hours trying not to fall asleep.)

So there I'd stood, on the steps outside church, when I spotted Pete down on the sidewalk, and at the top of my lungs I had hollered, "Hey, Taki! Let's call it Scramble!"

I hadn't done it on purpose; it just spilled out. But the words were barely out of my mouth when I knew I'd made a horrible mistake. Nobody except the grown-ups were allowed to call Pete "Taki" anymore. He'd never actually said that, but he didn't have to. Would *you* want other kids calling you a baby name like Taki once you're out of kindergarten?

Pete froze when he heard me holler that name, and his face went red.

I gulped.

But what could he do to me? We were still at church. There was a whole crowd of people around, and none of them thought twice about one kid hollering for another kid, or about hearing the name Taki. There were probably twenty fellas in the crowd at that moment named Panagiotakis. And I'd bet you dollars to donuts that every single one of their mothers and fathers called *them* Taki too. That's the way it goes if you're Greek. If you live to be a hundred, your 120-year-old ma will still call you by your baby name.

But between you and fellas your age, it's a different story. No one calls me Nicky, for example—at least, they'd better not. And no one calls Pete "Taki." The difference is, only one of us would actually haul off and punch someone for doing it.

So I knew I was asking for it, as soon as the words came out of my mouth.

Pete had stopped dead in his tracks when he heard that name. He turned, searching for the culprit, and then he eyed me on the church steps. He plowed toward me through the crowd of people on the sidewalk. Hats bobbed and ladies yelped as Pete swam upstream with vengeance in his eyes.

I stood there, like an idiot. Because even though I knew I had it coming, half of me still couldn't believe that Pete would sock someone in front of a zillion witnesses. On the steps of the church, no less.

That's when he swung at me.

But just because you know it's coming doesn't mean you have to stand there and take it. My survival instinct kicked in, and I ducked out of the way just in time.

With nothing for his fist to land on, Pete was thrown off balance. He spun around on his heels, and when his face came into view again, something *really* surprising happened.

I punched him right in the nose.

It wasn't a hard punch. I'd never hit anyone in my life before then, and my arms were as skinny as pipe cleaners. But it was enough to draw a trickle of blood from his nose. I don't know who was more surprised: Pete or me.

My folks had wandered off somewhere, so they hadn't seen it, thank goodness. And nobody else was paying any attention to two second graders on the steps of the church. They'd all been there long enough, and wanted to get home to take the Sunday dinner out of the oven.

But Pete's ma—remember the Queen of England?— she was down there on the sidewalk, busy talking to some other lady and paying no attention to us. At least, not while Pete took his swing (of course). But by the time I swung my skinny arm around and into Pete's nose, she had decided to look up. And (of course) she saw me land my punch. All of a sudden, her face went just as red as Pete's.

Now that I think about it, that might explain why Her Majesty does not like me.

Pete and me came to an unspoken understanding that day: I don't call him Taki, and he doesn't try to beat me up. It's a truce that's held for four years, so far. That's what I had to remind him about the other night, when I hollered at him in Greek from Ace's bedroom window. I wanted to keep it between me and him (for now), so I told Pete (in Greek) that if he didn't stop hassling me and Ace, I'd call him Taki loud and clear, right in front of everybody at Orchard Field, and

I dared him to try to punch me again. Because Pete's still bigger than me, but my arms aren't pipe cleaners anymore, and we both know it.

But Pete never could leave well enough alone. The next morning in church, there he was, with his face washed and his hair slicked down, looking like a decent human being. But he wasn't fooling me.

And then, sure enough, he managed to sneak up behind me as everyone was shuffling toward the doors after church.

"Just you wait, Spirakis," he hissed into my ear. "I'm gonna wipe the field with you next Saturday. You won't know what hit you."

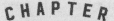

CHAPTER

27

*O*N SUNDAY AFTERNOON, Ma tuned in to *Polka Party* on the radio and Pop settled into his easy chair with the newspaper. I spread out the Sunday comics on the rug, and Uncle Spiro took the Sports page.

Pop eyed Spiro over the top of his newspaper. "You have no important places to go today?"

"Nah," said Spiro, yawning. "No school on Sunday."

"So why you couldn't come to church?" Pop said. "Sophia Costas, she ask about you again today."

Spiro didn't answer. He just said, "Hey, how about those Mudpuppies? They won two out of three games at Sheboygan."

"What's wrong with Sophia Costas?" said Pop.

Spiro didn't look up. "Nothing. She's a very lovely girl. She's just not my type."

"No one is your type," Pop grumbled. He rattled his newspaper. "Look, Nicky! Mister Joe Daggett is in the paper again."

I glanced up from reading *Superman*. "What's it say today?" Joe Daggett was in the newspaper a lot lately, what with all the activity at the ballpark since he came to town. The Pups had even managed to win a few games on their current road trip. But then I remembered: Spiro had the Sports section right now. So what was Pop reading?

I squinted at the newspaper in Pop's hands. It was the City section.

"Listen to this," said Pop. "'The Mudpuppies will host the ever-popular annual Zoo Spring Opening in a special pregame ceremony at Orchard Field on Saturday. A caravan of zoo animals will parade from the zoo to the Orchard and back again.' That Mister Daggett," said Pop, chuckling to himself. "He really knows how to have the fun."

"You go to the big day at the zoo every year, *neh*, Nicky?" said Ma from her chair. Her eyes were closed, and she was tapping her foot to the "Too Fat Polka."

"That's right," I said. "It's a swell time." Of course, I had to act like I hadn't heard Joe Daggett talk about the whole thing yesterday at the contest.

All this sneaking around was getting to be a lot of

trouble. For one thing, I had to try to remember what I was (or wasn't) supposed to know about stuff like this. And now I needed to think up another lie to get out of work for the second straight Saturday. I snuck a peek at Uncle Spiro. He might be my only chance. But he was hiding behind his newspaper.

"There's more," said Pop. "'As part of the pregame festivities, the winner of the first annual Mudpuppy for a Day Batboy Contest will be announced.'"

Now Uncle Spiro cocked an eyebrow at me over his newspaper.

Pop didn't notice. He just kept reading. "'"Saturday will be a memorable day for Pups fans," says owner Daggett. In addition, he announced that Saturday will be Ladies' Day at Orchard Field. Half price for the ladies that day.'"

"Ladies' Day?" said Ma, opening her eyes.

"I gave that idea to Mister Daggett," said Pop, puffing out his chest. "Remember that, Nicky?"

"I sure do, Pop." Credit where credit is due.

"It might be nice to see a ball game again sometime," said Ma, almost to herself.

Pop kept reading. "It says here: 'Get your tickets early, folks! Saturday promises to be a big—see next page—day at the Ol' Orchard!' Look here, Nicky. They talk about the contest yesterday too. When you were gone on your field trip to the state capitol."

"State capitol?" said Spiro. He was really giving me the stink-eye now.

"That's right," said Pop. "Nicky knows the education is important."

"What's it say, Pop?" I squeaked, trying not to look in Spiro's direction.

Pop pushed his glasses up on his nose. "'The contest was a rousing success,'" he read. "'Rousing,' it means 'good,' *neh*? It says: 'Saturday's outing drew hundreds of lads from all over the city, vying for a chance to be Mudpuppy for a Day.' What means 'vying'?"

I thought about it for a second. "Competing."

Pop nodded thoughtfully, and I imagined him tucking the word away into the filing cabinet of his brain.

I cleared my throat. "What else does it say?" I needed to keep Pop talking, so Spiro couldn't interrupt and ask about my "field trip" on Saturday.

"Let's see . . . ," said Pop, finding his place again. "Here it is: '"We sure do have a great bunch of kids in this town," said Daggett. "They showed true spirit and gump-tie-on out there at the ballpark."' Gump-tie-on?" asked Pop, spelling it out for me.

"Gumption," I told him. "It's like . . . courage, I guess. Nerve."

"I know someone with a lot of gumption," said Spiro from behind his paper.

Pop paid no attention. "It says here: 'Six finalists will compete for the honor: three winners of the field contest, and three essay winners.' Good for Mister Daggett! He knows the reading and writing are important. A very smart man." He kept reading. "'The three field-contest finalists were identified as . . .'"

I froze on the carpet. In the funny papers, Prince Valiant sneered up at me from under his pageboy haircut.

Then Pop read, "'See next page . . .'"

I couldn't breathe.

It took Pop maybe two seconds to flip the page and find his place again, but those two seconds were the longest of my entire life.

Pop would see my name. He'd know I lied about the field trip.

I was doomed.

"What is this?" said Pop, adjusting his glasses.

Here it came. My life was over.

But then Pop did something I wasn't expecting in a million years. He smiled. "Look, Nicky! Peter Costas of Cherry Street is one of the winners! That's your friend Taki, *neh*?"

"Yep," I squeaked. (By the way, see what I mean about grown-ups calling you by your baby name forever?)

"Pete Costas?" said Spiro, eyeing me with suspicion.

This was not going well. I held my breath, waiting for

Pop to read my name and bracing for whatever might come next.

But he didn't read my name, or anything else out loud. He just scanned a bit more, silently, and then folded the paper and handed it to me. "See your friend's name?" Then he picked up another section of the Sunday paper, sat back in his easy chair, and started reading. "It says here that rain is coming on Tuesday. . . ."

But I'd stopped listening. Why hadn't Pop gotten mad about seeing my name? I hadn't dreamed yesterday, had I? It had all seemed pretty darn real: Joe Daggett calling me down onto the infield with Pete and some other kid from the east side named Wayne. I looked down now and scanned the page that Pop had given me. There were the names:

> Peter Costas, West Cherry Street
> Wayne Stanke, East Walnut Street
> Mick Sparks, North Forty-Fourth Street

It took me a second or two, but then all of a sudden, it made sense.

I was Mick Sparks.

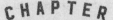

CHAPTER

28

$\mathcal{S}$AY, POP, DO YA MIND if I take this over and show it to Ace?" I said, as casually as I could. "He'll, uh, wanna see Pete's name too."

"I don't mind," said Pop, settling into his chair for a nap.

Before Uncle Spiro could say anything, I folded up the City section and headed out to the front hall to put on my shoes.

But I couldn't tie them fast enough.

"All right, squirt." It was Uncle Spiro, standing in the doorway. "What gives?"

"Huh?" I squeaked as I took my ball cap off the hook.

"Big contest out at Orchard Field yesterday, eh? Mudpuppy for a Day? Seems to me I heard something about that recently. How *somebody* was gonna clean Pete's clock. How'd that work out?"

I didn't say anything. I'd listened to enough episodes of *Dick Tracy* to know that my uncle couldn't make me testify against myself.

Spiro stuck his hands in his pockets and looked at the ceiling. "Of course, *you* wouldn't know anything about that. Because you work in your pop's shop on Saturdays. Or—no, wait a minute—you went on a field trip to the state capitol, isn't that it? A school field trip, all the way to Madison. And on a Saturday too. What a coincidence." He gave me a wicked grin and unwrapped a stick of licorice gum.

"Knock it off," I muttered. "I gotta go."

"Not so fast, sport." He chomped his gum. "I seem to remember somebody blackmailing me pretty good the other day. It's payback time."

I made a move for the front door, but Uncle Spiro blocked it with his foot.

"Okay, fine!" I looked past him to where Ma and Pop were snoozing. "Can we at least go outside first?"

So we went out to the front porch. It was a pretty day, the first really warm day of spring, and the elm trees were leafing out, forming a cool, green tunnel over the street.

Too bad my life was over.

I plopped down onto the porch steps. Uncle Spiro sat

next to me and held out a stick of gum. I took it, unwrapped it, and started chewing.

"Yuck!" I said, looking up in surprise. "How can you chew this stuff? It tastes like medicine."

He laughed and chomped his own gum. "It grows on you."

I sat there, choking down that awful licorice flavor and staring up at the trees. I knew he was waiting for me to start talking. Might as well get it over with.

"You have to promise not to tell," I started off.

Uncle Spiro gave a fake gasp. "Who, me?" Then he softened up when he saw I was serious. "Okay, I promise," he said.

"Pop will kill me."

Uncle Spiro rested his arms across his knees. "Listen, kid, I have a feeling I've done stuff a million times worse, and he hasn't killed me yet. But how's he gonna know, if we don't tell him? Let me guess: You didn't go on a field trip to Madison yesterday."

"Nope."

"Did you go down to Orchard Field?"

I nodded.

Spiro nodded too. "All that trouble, cooking up a story to tell your pop so you could get out of work, and what do ya get? Your ol' nemesis Pete wins a finalist spot instead of you." He patted me on the back. "I know it stinks, kid. But at least you tried. And I understand why you couldn't tell your pop. Your secret's safe with me."

For half a second I thought about stopping there. Uncle Spiro was being nice and everything, but I reminded myself again that he was still a grown-up.

But then I realized that I *wanted* to tell him more. Here I was, one of three finalists from yesterday. One of only six kids in the whole city who would compete for the big prize. And who could I tell? Nobody. Even the newspaper got my name wrong. I was completely anonymous, and I couldn't stand it.

"That's not all," I told Uncle Spiro. I handed him the newspaper. "I'm a finalist too."

He stopped chewing his gum and stared at me.

So I pointed to the list of names. "See that last name, Mick Sparks?" I tapped the page. "That's me."

Spiro frowned at the newspaper. Then his eyebrows shot up, and he broke into a grin. "Mick Sparks! You're a finalist?"

"Shhh!" I said, looking over my shoulder. "They called my number yesterday, so I know for sure it's me. I guess my penmanship needs work."

"Well, if that don't beat all," said Spiro, clapping me on the back. But then his smile faded. "Wait a minute. You can't tell your folks, can you?"

I shook my head. "If I do, they'll know I lied."

"That stinks."

"I know."

We sat in silence for a minute. Finally Uncle Spiro said, "So, when's the big day?"

"Next Saturday," I told him.

"Another Saturday, huh?"

I nodded. "I didn't think I'd have to worry about it. I didn't expect to win." And then I decided to ask him, before I lost my nerve.

"I don't suppose you'd be willing to—"

Spiro held up a hand before I could finish. "Sorry, kid. Don't ask. I already have big plans of my own that day, and I can't change 'em."

"Like what?"

He watched a pair of kids ride past on their bikes. "I can't say."

"What?" I yelped. "After everything I just told you?"

He shrugged. "Sorry. You gotta trust me."

I hopped up onto my feet. "I told you *everything*. Even stuff I didn't have to tell you. And you know what a big deal this is! I bet you got nowhere to go, and nothing to do. You don't even go to school! Pop is right about you! You're just shifty and selfish and a—a freeloader!"

"Now just you hold on!" said Spiro, and for maybe only the second time in my life, I heard anger in his voice.

But I didn't care. I was mad too. I stomped down the porch steps and ran over to Ace's house with the newspaper. At least *he'd* be happy for Mick Sparks.

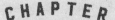

CHAPTER 29

I LEANED ON ACE'S DOORBELL, and almost let myself into the house so I wouldn't have to feel Spiro's deadly stare.

Finally the door swung open, and there was Ace. His hair was all messed up, and he was still in his pajamas.

"What's up with you?" I asked him, pushing my way into the house. "Are you sick?"

"Nah. But my ma is being nice to me on account of my broken arm. She let me sleep in." He yawned and scratched his wrist where it stuck out of his muddy cast.

"That thing is disgusting," I told him. "How are you gonna stand it for six whole weeks?"

Ace inspected his cast. "I like it. It has personality."

"It's gonna smell like it has its own personality pretty soon."

"Very funny," he said. "So what's going on with you today? Wanna play Monopoly or something?" Behind him, his pop and little sister were at the dining room table, setting up the game. I could hear "Chattanooga Choo Choo" playing on the radio.

"No thanks," I said. "Your sister cheats."

"That's what I tried to tell my pop."

Just then, we heard a car horn outside.

"Sounds like the Nash," I said, frowning.

Me and Ace pushed the curtain aside, and sure enough, there was Uncle Spiro out front, laying on the horn.

"Your uncle wants you," said Ace helpfully.

I sighed.

The horn honked again.

"Aren't ya gonna see what he wants?" said Ace.

I jammed my hands in my pockets, thinking. Then I said, "Come with me. Maybe he won't kill me in front of you."

Ace perked up at this. "What did you do?"

"Nothing," I muttered. "I might have called him rude names. But he deserved it! He still won't cover for me next Saturday, even though he knows how important it is."

The car horn honked again.

"Horace?" called Ace's pop, looking up from the Monopoly game. "Who's that beeping on a Sunday afternoon? How am I supposed to concentrate? I just landed on Boardwalk."

Ace's little sister gave an evil laugh. She already had her victim in her sights.

"I'll go check, Pop," called Ace as we went outside.

Uncle Spiro stopped honking when he saw us come out of the house. "Get in," he said through the open car window. He did not look happy.

I hesitated. "Can Ace come?" I might need a witness.

Spiro looked Ace up and down, taking in the messy hair, striped pajamas, scuffed slippers, and grimy cast.

"What'd you do to your arm?" said Spiro, chomping his gum.

Ace held out his cast. "Broke it."

"Oh," said Spiro. He wrinkled his nose. "It's disgusting."

"Thanks!"

"Okay, you two knuckleheads, get in."

Me and Ace climbed into the back seat, and Uncle Spiro pulled away from the curb. I was almost afraid to ask, but I said, "Where are we going?"

"For frozen custard," said Spiro.

Ace nudged me and whispered, "I thought he was sore at you."

I just shrugged.

We rode in silence as Uncle Spiro drove past Roger's custard stand. That was no big deal. Sometimes you just have a taste for Happy's custard. But when he drove past Happy's, too, me and Ace looked at each other, trying to figure out what he was up to.

Finally, I couldn't stand it. I leaned forward and tapped Uncle Spiro on the shoulder. "Uh, where are we going? We just drove past the only two custard stands on this side of town."

"We're almost there," was all he said.

A minute later, Uncle Spiro pulled the Nash to the curb and parked. "Here we are," he said, getting out of the car. "Come on."

We got out of the car too, and followed Spiro down the sidewalk for half a block. Then he stopped in front of a small building, all white, glossy-painted brick with red trim. It had a glass door with a **CLOSED** sign dangling on the inside, and big windows across the front. There were two picnic tables out front, also painted red, and a billboard that said:

COMING SOON!
THE BEST FROZEN CUSTARD IN TOWN

Spiro stood looking at the building, hands on hips. "Well?" he said. "What ya think?"

Me and Ace looked at each other, frowning.

"You're taking us for custard here?" I said. "It's not even open yet."

"I know," said Spiro, chewing his gum and wiggling his eyebrows. "Grand opening is next Saturday."

I scratched my head. "Next Saturday? The twenty-ninth?"

"That's the big day at the ballpark," said Ace, nudging me. "Mudpuppy for a Day. Zoo parade. The whole shebang."

Uncle Spiro looked at us with a huge grin on his face. "I've been trying to figure out what to call it," he said. "'Spiro's Custard' doesn't have the right ring to it. And then you gave me an idea for the perfect name."

My mouth dropped open.

"What do you think about this?" he said, framing the little white building with his outstretched hands. "'Sparky's Custard.'"

30

*T*WENTY MINUTES LATER, we sat at one of the picnic tables, slurping our cones. Spiro had given us a whole tour. He showed us how the custard machines worked, and even let us fill our own cones. He had a soda fountain too, and a cash register, and a jukebox, and everything. He even had a little bell on the door just like Pop's hat shop.

"How do you like it?" said Spiro as we licked our cones.

"This is the most delicious custard I've ever eaten in my entire life," I said, my voice all chocolatey and sticky. "And the shop is pretty great too."

Ace nodded. "This chocolate is even better than the vanilla. But I might need another taste of that, just to be sure." He had managed to dribble both flavors onto his cast.

Spiro looked around and nodded. "I think I'm gonna do

okay. I'm only two blocks from Orchard Field. I ought to do pretty good business on game days."

I put my feet up on the picnic table bench and grunted. "So how come the big secret?" I asked him finally. "Don't you think Pop will be happy to see you opening your own business?"

Uncle Spiro straightened the napkin holder on the table. "I think so," he said. "But it just seems easier this way. He'd have been full of all kinds of advice, and telling me how *he* would do things. Not that he doesn't have good ideas, but this was something I needed to do on my own, ya know?"

I did know.

"Besides," said Spiro. "Now I can surprise him."

"Where'd you learn about custard and stuff?" said Ace, who was clearly impressed.

"I spent six months apprenticing down at South Side Lenny's," said Uncle Spiro.

Ace nudged me. "That's why we saw him driving south over the viaduct that night!"

Spiro kept going. "Lenny and me were in the army together. He was a mess cook in France, just like me. He told me I had a knack for food. And I liked it. So, once the war was over and we came back home, I asked him to teach me everything he knew. He's way down on the south side, so I won't compete with him for customers."

I crunched the last of my cone. "So that's why you were out so late every night?"

Spiro nodded. "I had to learn the whole business from the ground up, including cleaning up after closing time. And then, I did go to night school for a while. Took some classes down at the technical college. Bookkeeping and stuff like that."

I looked at my uncle. It all made sense now, of course. The sneaking around. The excuses for not being able to work in Pop's shop. The custard taste tests. I wiped my sticky face with a napkin. "I'm sorry I called you a shifty freeloader."

Spiro laughed and rubbed my crew cut. "That's all right, squirt. And don't worry. We'll figure out something for next Saturday."

"Yeah," I said. "I need to think about that." I picked at a splinter in the picnic table.

"Well," Spiro said, "you could always come clean."

"I dunno. . . ."

Ace piped up. "He'll probably find out sooner or later. And what happens if you actually win the big contest? Don't you want your folks there to see it?" He was right. I hated that.

But I wasn't quite ready to do it. "I'll think about it," I said. "Hey, Uncle Spiro. Can we try the soda fountain?"

"Sure thing, Sparky."

CHAPTER

31

*F*ROM THAT DAY ON, my nickname at school was Mick Sparks. Half the kids didn't believe that was me in the newspaper, and the other half thought it was hilarious and wouldn't call me anything else. Pete was no help. "I don't know who this Mick Sparks fella is," he'd say, with an evil glint in his eye, "but I'm gonna wipe the field with him on Saturday."

And then, instead of playing Scramble, we all retreated to our opposite corners of the zoo to strategize for Saturday's final contest. Pete was convinced it was finally gonna be traditional baseball skills. But me and Ace weren't so sure. We knew Joe Daggett better than that. Whatever he had up his sleeve, it would probably be something you couldn't practice for.

"I hope it has something to do with the monkeys," said Ace as we walked home from school on Wednesday. "Maybe they'll let the monkeys loose on the field, and whoever can wrangle the most, wins."

"That's what I like about you, Ace," I told him, kicking a pebble down the sidewalk. "You're a very optimistic person."

When we got to Mountain Goat Mountain, Penny was waiting for us, all breathless. Her hair was even more wild than usual, and her socks were bunched down around the tops of her saddle shoes.

"Look!" she called, waving us over. "It was waiting for me when I got home from school! I ran all the way here." She held out an envelope. "Look!"

"Hey!" said Ace. "It's from the Mudpuppies Baseball Club!"

"It's on official Mudpuppies stationery and everything," she said. "And it's addressed to me!" She opened the letter and read it out loud.

> *"Dear Miss Lonergan,*
> *Thank you for submitting your essay to the First Annual Mudpuppy for a Day Batboy Contest. You were the only young lady to submit an essay."*

"They read it!" I said. "That's great!"
"I know," said Penny. "Listen to this.

*"The Mudpuppies Baseball Club takes seriously our
responsibility to preserve and protect the delicate
sensibilities of our fans of the fairer sex. As a result,
young ladies are precluded from entering the
contest."*

"Hold it," I said. "What the heck does all that mean?"

Penny wrinkled her nose. "It means that I'm too delicate
to compete."

"You?" Ace snorted. "Shows you what they know."

"I don't get it," said Penny. "It's not like a batboy has to
lift a hundred pounds or anything."

Me and Ace both shrugged. Penny was right: It didn't
make any sense. But apparently it was the rule, and every kid
knows that some rules exist for only one reason: to make life
easier for grown-ups. Nine o'clock bedtime, for example. Or
"Keep out of the rhino pen." Any way you looked at it, the
"no girls" rule sounded like one of those.

"Wait, there's more." Penny cleared her throat and kept
reading.

*"However, after reading all the submissions, the
judging panel unanimously agreed that yours was
the best essay we received. It displayed creativity,
enthusiasm, impressive knowledge of baseball, and
perfect spelling, all in exactly one hundred words."*

Me and Ace both whooped and hollered when we heard that.

Penny just grinned, and she kept reading.

> *"In recognition of this outstanding achievement, we would like to invite you to be our guest on Saturday, May 29, to receive a special award during our pregame ceremonies. Please visit the Mudpuppies executive offices at your earliest convenience to collect free game tickets for you and a friend.*
>
> *Best wishes,*
>
> *J P Daggett*
>
> *Joseph P. Daggett*
> *President, Mudpuppies Baseball Club"*

Penny showed us Joe Daggett's signature. Then she folded the letter and put it back in the envelope.

"Jeepers," I said.

"That Joe Daggett is one okay fella," said Ace.

Penny was beaming. "I'm gonna see if Josie can come up from Kenosha for the game," she said.

"We all get to go to the game on Saturday," I said. "How great is that?"

"When are you gonna pick up your tickets?" said Ace.

Penny pushed her hair out of her face. "How about right now? Wanna come with me? You said you know Mr. Daggett."

Me and Ace both held up our crossed fingers. "We're like this."

CHAPTER

32

$\mathcal{W}$E TOOK THE STREETCAR to Orchard Field and walked straight to the Mudpuppies office. But before I could knock on the door, Ace turned the knob and busted in like he owned the place.

There was ol' Miss Garble at her desk, jumping in surprise and dropping a lit cigarette into her lap.

"Oh, it's you again," she said, patting at her skirt before it could catch fire. A cloud of smoke drifted around her.

"That's right," said Ace, smooth as glass. "We're here to see Joe Daggett."

Miss Garble glanced toward the closed door of the inner office. "He's on the phone."

From the other side of the door, we could hear a loud voice.

"I'm sorry, Bill," Joe Daggett was saying, "but we're gonna have to return all these jars of mustard. Everybody knows you can't put yellow mustard on a hot dog! It's spicy brown or nothing. Well, it can't be nothing. What's a hot dog without mustard, am I right? No, Bill, I need it before the home stand this weekend. Trust me, you'll taste a difference!"

We heard a *klunk* and then Joe Daggett hollered, "Miss Garble!"

She crushed her cigarette in the ashtray on her desk, rubbed her forehead, and went to open the inner office door. "Yes, Mr. Daggett?"

"Miss Garble, Bill from food service will be along shortly to switch out twelve dozen gallon-sized jars of mustard. Can you show him to the concession office when he gets here?"

Miss Garble smiled weakly. "Of course, Mr. Daggett. Oh, Mr. Daggett? There are some, uh, young gentlemen and"— she looked Penny up and down to make sure, I guess—"a young lady here to see you."

"Show 'em in!" he said.

Miss Garble held the door open and gestured for us to go in.

"Well, howdy kids!" said Joe Daggett from behind a giant metal desk piled with papers. In the middle of all the paper sat a gallon-sized jar of yellow mustard. Joe Daggett had his feet up on the desk, on top of all the papers. He had black-and-yellow argyle socks on both feet. I guess Joe Daggett dressed up for the office.

He reached across his desk to shake our hands. "Nice to see you fellas again! Nick, am I right? And"—he snapped his fingers, thinking—"Ace! Say, what happened to your arm?"

Ace showed off his cast. "Raced a rhino. I won."

"Thank goodness," said Joe Daggett. "And who's this young lady?"

"This is our friend Penny," I said.

Joe Daggett tipped his imaginary hat. "Hello, Penny. Glad you kids stopped by. My door is always open. Except when it's closed, ha! But that's just because I like to make Miss Garble wonder what's going on in here. Keeps her on her toes. What can I do for you?"

Penny pulled Joe Daggett's letter out of her skirt. (Apparently she had pockets in there somewhere.) "It's about this," she said, handing the envelope to Joe Daggett.

He scanned the letter, and his eyebrows shot up. "You're Penny Lonergan? Congratulations, young lady! Let me shake your hand!"

He dragged his feet off his desk, sending papers sliding to the floor and almost knocking over the giant jar of yellow mustard. Then he stood up and pumped Penny's hand. "Miss Garble!" he hollered.

Miss Garble appeared in the doorway again. "Yes, Mr. Daggett?"

"Miss Garble, this is Penny Lonergan! We were all very impressed with Penny's essay, weren't we, Miss Garble?"

"That's right," said Miss Garble. "And I ought to know. I read every single one."

"Oh, it wasn't that bad," said Joe Daggett.

Ace sidled up to Miss Garble. "How did you like my seventeen-page masterpiece?"

Miss Garble took a step backward and peered at Ace over her glasses. "That was you?"

"We have tickets for you, Penny," said Joe Daggett. He rummaged around the piles of paper on his desk. "Miss Garble, have you seen—?"

"Right here, Mr. Daggett." Without blinking an eye, Miss Garble fished a small envelope out of the pile and handed it to Penny. Then she left the room, shaking her head.

Penny opened the envelope and gasped. "Section One, Row One?"

Joe Daggett winked. "Two seats, directly behind home plate." He perched on the edge of his desk and grinned. "And I hope you'll take part in our pregame ceremonies too. After the zoo caravan, we're going to announce the big winner of the batboy contest. And then I'd like to introduce our very special, honorary essay winner. What do ya say?"

"Gee, thanks, Mr. Daggett," said Penny, but she didn't

sound as excited as I thought she'd be. "Can I ask you a question, though? I mean, this is all really nice of you, but I wonder: Do you really believe what you said here?" She took the letter from Joe Daggett and studied it. "This part here," she said, pointing, "about preserving and protecting the . . . 'delicate sensibilities . . . of the fairer sex'? We're not babies. We're girls. Why can't girls do stuff too?"

"Girls?" said Joe Daggett, lifting his eyebrows. He rubbed his knee, thinking. "Girls," he said again to himself. Then he snapped his fingers. "It'll be Ladies' Day on Saturday. Half price admission."

Penny cleared her throat. "I was thinking that girls could actually *do* something, besides watch. For instance, the batboy contest." She shifted on her feet. "How come girls are"—she searched the letter again—"'precluded from entering the contest'? That means not allowed to be a batboy, right? But how come? And you can't say it's because the word 'batboy' has 'boy' in it," she added quickly. "I mean, I know the finalists are already decided. But . . . maybe you could think about including girls next time?"

Joe Daggett scratched his head. "You think that's a good idea?"

"Yes, sir," said Penny. "Girls even *play* baseball, you know. Have you heard of the AAGPBL?"

Joe Daggett's eyebrows went up. "Sure I have."

"What's the A-A-G-Peeble?" said Ace.

I shrugged. I didn't know either.

"It's the All-American Girls' Professional Baseball League," said Joe Daggett. "Ten teams, I think, here in the upper Midwest. I'm told they're even pitching overhand this year."

Penny nodded. "They're good players too. Me and my dad drive down to watch whenever there's a game in Kenosha or Racine."

"Is that so?" said Joe Daggett. "You got a favorite player?"

"Josie Lonergan," said Penny, without missing a beat. "She plays shortstop for the Kenosha Comets."

My mouth dropped open. "Wait a minute. Josie *Lonergan*?"

"Your sister is a *ballplayer*?" said Ace.

"Yep," said Penny proudly.

A big grin spread across Joe Daggett's face. "Well, if that don't beat all. Miss Garble!"

We heard footsteps, and here came ol' Miss Garble again. "Yes, Mr. Daggett?" A fresh cigarette was in her hand, sending up a thin swirl of blue smoke.

"Miss Garble, how many times have I told you? That stuff'll kill you!"

Miss Garble looked hurt. "But Mr. Daggett, you know what the magazine ads say. More doctors smoke Camels than any other cigarette." She coughed.

"And I thought *I* was a huckster," Joe Daggett said to

me out of the corner of his mouth. "Miss Garble, that's the fattest load of hooey I've ever heard. Now put out that noxious thing and make a phone call for me, will you? I need to speak to the front office of the Kenosha Comets Baseball Club, toot sweet. Ask the long distance operator for the number." He folded his arms across his chest and grinned. "Let's add one more feature to Saturday's pre-game ceremony. I'm going to invite the shortstop of the Kenosha Comets to throw out the first pitch!"

33

*H*ow about that?" said Ace as the three of us crammed into a seat on the streetcar headed home. "Your sister's a professional ballplayer!"

"I know that," said Penny, but she had a big grin on her face.

"How come you never told us?" I asked.

Penny shrugged. "I never know what somebody is gonna say. Most of the time, people think it's neat. But some people say it's not ladylike." Penny blushed, and she leaned close so she could whisper. "One lady told Josie that if she kept playing ball, she'd never be able to have babies."

I have to admit: I'm not too swift on the female anatomy, though you can't say I haven't tried. One time I happened to find a cheesecake magazine in Uncle Spiro's room, but I only got a peek at a leg and some garters before he walked in and hollered at me to get out of his room forever. Gee whiz. Anyhow, despite my lack of knowledge in that department, I was pretty sure that playing ball and having babies involved completely different body parts. "I don't get it," I said.

"Me either," said Penny. Now she was blushing bright red. "Even my mom says it's dumb."

"Anyhow, me and Ace think it's pretty swell that your sister plays ball," I said. "Don't we, Ace?"

He nodded. "You bet! And now Joe Daggett invited her to the game on Saturday! You'll be on the field with your sister! And sit behind home plate! Those tickets cost a dollar fifty each!"

A smile bloomed on Penny's face. "I never expected that to happen."

"Now we know why you're such a good ballplayer," I told Penny. "It runs in your family."

Penny shrugged. "Josie practices with me in the off-season. She's taught me a lot. She even taught me how to pitch overhand, so she could get some good batting practice."

Which got me thinking. Penny had been planning to enter the contest all along, but she'd still offered to coach me. Which just proves again that Penny's okay, even though she's a girl. "Hey, thanks for helping me with stuff. I'd never be ready for Saturday if it wasn't for your help."

Penny looked at me out of the corner of her eye. "You think that'll be the final contest? Catching fly balls?"

"My money's still on monkeys," said Ace. "Let 'em loose, and chase 'em down."

"I dunno," I said, ignoring Ace. "But maybe."

"If it is, you'll do great. It's all up here," Penny said, tapping her head. "That's what Josie says, anyway. And don't ever take your eye off the ball."

"That sounds easy," said Ace, wiggling a finger up under his cast to scratch an itch.

"Oh, sure, it *sounds* easy," I said.

"You're a good player," Penny said. "You're getting the hang of it." Then she gave me a wicked smile. "Besides, you can't let Pete win."

"Thanks," I said. Like I said: Penny's pretty swell, for a girl.

CHAPTER 34

*B*UT WE COULDN'T PRACTICE at the zoo the next day. The whole place was crawling with zookeepers getting everything ready for the big Spring Opening, which was only two days away. That meant the animals would be officially released outside for the whole summer, so their outdoor spaces had to be cleaned. Zookeepers in big rubber boots hosed down the empty enclosures and scrubbed them with stiff brooms. Then they scattered fresh bales of hay for the elephant, and the giraffes, and the zebra. Even Tank got some fresh hay, and he slept through the whole thing. Sometimes he can be pretty calm, for a rhino.

Over at Monkey Island, we watched one fella launching a wooden rowboat into the moat, and another fella hanging up a brand new tire swing.

"Do the monkeys go in the water?" asked Penny as we watched from the edge of the moat. She was still pretty new in town, so she hadn't seen the monkeys outside yet.

"You bet!" said Ace. "They're really good swimmers. It's hilarious."

"They swim over to the rowboat and climb in," I said. "There's no oars or anything, but they like to float around. And then they jump into the water."

Penny leaned over the low wall and dipped her fingers into the water of the moat. "I could reach out and touch a swimming monkey?" she said.

"You could, but trust me, you don't want to," said Ace. "They bite." I won't go into details right now, but let's just say he knows from experience.

"Can't they climb out?" said Penny, taking a step backward. "I mean, this wall isn't very high. If they can climb into the rowboat . . ."

I shrugged. "I don't know why they don't climb out, but they never do. I guess the wall is too smooth for them, maybe."

"And the water gets deeper here, next to the wall," said Ace. (He knows that from experience too.) "The monkeys can't climb out if they can't touch the bottom. A zookeeper told me that while he was pulling me out of the moat." He gave Penny a crooked grin, and his ears went red. "It was an accident."

Penny shook her head. "This is a crazy zoo. Monkeys close enough to touch. Mountain goats afraid of *you* instead of the other way around. The rhinoceros fence only this high." She held a hand up to her waist. Then she looked at me and Ace. "Or maybe it's *you guys* that are crazy. Climbing in with dangerous animals like it's no big deal!"

Ace held up his disgustingly dirty cast like it was a trophy. "See this scar on my thumb? Monkey bite."

I just smiled and said, "It's the most wonderful place in the whole wide world."

⚾ ⚾ ⚾

Since we couldn't practice at the zoo, we went back to school and used the playground. It's a good place to practice baseball, because there's lots of room, and there's a high fence along one side. But it's also bad, because it's all pavement, which is nasty if you trip and fall. And also, lots of other kids use the playground after school, so there's always somebody watching you, and I've already described how an audience makes me really nervous.

But with all the activity at the zoo, we didn't have much choice.

At least Pete and his gang steered clear. I don't know if either me or Pete thought that I'd have the guts to risk a punch in the face by calling him Taki in front of everybody, but I guess he decided not to find out. Which was fine by me.

We claimed our territory on the playground, and Ace pitched. He did pretty good too, considering he had a cast on one arm. Penny was the batter, and I played right field. (Since she's a lefty, that's where she hit the ball most of the time.)

I practiced "reading" the ball, just like Penny had shown me at Mountain Goat Mountain. And now that we had more room, Penny showed me how to run on the balls of your feet when you're chasing down a fly ball, instead of heel to toe. It felt really strange at first. But she said it's easier to see the ball that way, because your head doesn't bounce as much when you run. And she was right.

Sure enough, pretty soon I was able to catch a few really high ones, even with other kids watching. And the more fly balls I caught, the less nervous I got.

Things were starting to look up. If the final contest had anything to do with catching fly balls, I might actually have a chance on Saturday.

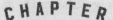

$\mathcal{T}$HAT NIGHT, there was a full-page ad in the newspaper, announcing the big day: The caravan of
animals from the zoo to Orchard Field and back again.
The Mudpuppy for a Day final contest. And (oh yeah)
the ball game. And the whole thing was even going to be
broadcast live on the radio. Joe Daggett had really gone
whole hog.

"Hey, Pop, did you see the map of the parade route?" I
told him at the supper table. "Right down Frederick Street.
It'll go past the shop!"

Pop nodded as he wiped his plate clean with a hunk of
bread. "You and I, we can watch it going past, *neh*?"

"Yep," I croaked. I still hadn't figured out a way to tell
him that I wouldn't be at the shop on Saturday. But I needed

to think of something pretty quick. Saturday was only two days away.

Uncle Spiro cleared his throat. "Lots going on at the ballpark on Saturday, that's for sure. Big parade. Marching bands. Quite a spectacle."

"And don't forget," said Ma, dabbing her mouth with her napkin, "Ladies' Day."

"You'll be able to listen to the whole thing on the radio, Ma," I told her. "While you're ironing and dusting and stuff."

She gave me a funny look—I don't know why. Then she got all dreamy and said, "Remember, George, how we used to go to the ball games? That was lots of fun, *neh*?"

Pop nodded. "The good old days!" he said.

"Nicky, I can't listen on the radio," said Ma with a sigh. "Ladies' Guild meeting at the church on Saturday. They are going to choose whose *koulouria* will be sold at the church bake sale."

"Of course they'll choose yours, Athena," said Uncle Spiro.

Ma shook her head. "That Mrs. Costas, she's very fussy."

"Who cares what ol' Mrs. Costas thinks, anyhow?" I said. "*We* know your cookies are the best, Ma." Poor Ma, having to put up with the Queen of England instead of hearing all the fun on the radio.

Uncle Spiro pushed his chair back and patted his

stomach with both hands. "If your cookies are even half as good as this dinner, Athena, you'll be a shoo-in."

Ma reached over and pinched Spiro's cheek. Some things you just never outgrow.

"I was thinking, George," said Spiro, rubbing his cheek. "With all the hullabaloo around town on Saturday, I bet it'll be pretty quiet at the shop."

Pop gave Spiro a suspicious look.

So did I.

But then Pop nodded and said, "Maybe you're right."

"Sure, I'm right," said Spiro. "Which would you rather do, if you were the average Joe? Get your shoes shined, or watch a wagonload of monkeys parade around the ball field?"

Pop chuckled to himself, and then he said, "Monkeys."

"Of course, monkeys," said Spiro. "So why not give Nicky the day off on Saturday? Let him go down to the ballpark and see all the hubbub. You won't need him at the shop."

My mouth dropped open. Uncle Spiro snuck me a quick wink.

Pop's smile faded, and his eyebrows scrunched together. He folded his napkin and laid it carefully on the table. He looked at Spiro, and then at me, and then at Ma.

"You know what, Spiro?" he said, shaking a finger at his brother. "Sometimes you have the very good ideas. Nicky?

Take the day off on Saturday. Go down to the ballpark and see the monkeys!"

I almost couldn't believe my ears. "Honest, Pop? That'd be the best!"

"Sure, sure," said Pop, waving a hand. "Go. Have fun."

"Gee thanks, Pop!" And just like that, my problem was solved.

Uncle Spiro gave me another wink. "It *will* be fun, George. In fact, I think *you* should go to the game on Saturday too. You could use a day off, if you ask me."

I tried to wave Spiro off. I mean, he was right: Pop deserved a day off now and then. But if Pop went to the game, he'd see me on the field, in the Mudpuppy for a Day contest. The jig would be up, and I'd be in trouble for sure.

But I should've known I didn't need to worry.

"That is what makes us different, Spiro," said Pop, leaning back in his chair. "I know how important is the hard work." He shook his finger again. "A man never gets anyplace without hard work."

Spiro sighed. "It's just one day, George. It won't kill you to close the shop for one day."

"Close the shop?" said Pop, looking horrified. "What happens if a customer comes to the shop and finds it closed? I tell you what happens: He goes to another shop, and he tells all his friends that the Elegant Shoe Repair and Hat Shop is now closed, so everybody else, they go to another shop too. There goes my whole business. Just because of a bunch of monkeys!"

Spiro was his usual calm self. "How about if I make you a nice sign to hang in the window, George? **CLOSED TODAY ONLY. GONE TO SEE THE MONKEYS.** If you ask me, no one would blame you. Maybe that would even get you new customers. People who appreciate someone with enough good sense to go see a ball game every now and then."

"You joke," said Pop, "but this is why I am a successful businessman and you are"—he thought for a second, and then he shrugged—"you are nothing. Going to the ball game and having fun is for the children, like Nicky. And you, maybe. But I have responsibilities. Saturday, it's a working day, and so *I* will be at work. Monkeys or no monkeys!"

Uncle Spiro shrugged. "Suit yourself, George. But I'll bet that no one comes to the shop on Saturday. Everyone will be at the ball game. *Everyone.*"

Pop folded his arms across his chest. "Everyone except me."

And that was the end of the discussion.

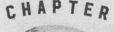

J WASN'T GOING TO LET all the arguing ruin my good mood. I was going to the Spring Opening festivities on Saturday, and I didn't even have to cheat, or lie, or anything. For once. I was so happy, I even volunteered to help Ma clean up the supper dishes.

"I gotta get going," said Uncle Spiro. "Thanks for supper, Athena." He grabbed the car keys from their hook and headed out the back door.

I followed him out to the alley. "Thanks."

He rubbed my crew cut. "Don't mention it, squirt. Besides, I meant it. Saturday's gonna be a swell day, and you should be there, without having to sneak around."

"It *will* be swell," I told him. "I wish you could come."

"Me too," he said. "But I can't change my plans now. Saturday's my grand opening!"

"You oughta do good business after the game," I said.

"That's the plan, Sparky," said Uncle Spiro. "I'm heading down there right now to give everything one last test run. Don't say anything to your folks yet, though. It's still a surprise."

"Even after Pop called you a nothing?"

He laughed as he opened the car door. "I guess now it'll be an even bigger surprise. Speaking of surprises, are you gonna tell them about the batboy contest? I bet they'd be pretty excited for you."

I shifted on my feet. "I dunno. I don't wanna get in trouble." So far, I'd gotten away with lying, and with forging Pop's signature. I didn't feel good about it, but my secret was safe. I was in the clear. All I had to do was keep my mouth shut, and they'd never know.

Except they'd never know I was a Mudpuppy for a Day finalist either, and I'd never be able to tell them, unless I wanted to be exposed for the devious cheating liar I really was.

But what could I do? Rule Number One when you're a kid: Stay out of trouble. Rule Number Two: If you can't follow Rule Number One, don't get caught.

I looked up at my uncle. "I guess we both have a

secret. I'll keep yours if you keep mine."

"If you're sure," said Spiro. I nodded, and so he slid into the Nash, started the engine, and chugged away down the alley.

I headed back inside to help Ma with the dishes like I'd promised.

"Nicky," she said to me as the back door banged shut. "I heard the front doorbell."

Pop was already behind his newspaper. "Must be the paperboy, collecting for the month," he said. "The money, it's on the hallway table, Nicky. Tell him to keep the change for his tip, *neh*?"

"Sure thing, Pop." The doorbell rang again, twice. "Hold your horses, Charlie!" I hollered, and headed out to the front hall. I found a dollar bill and two quarters on the hall table and opened the door.

"Hiya, Charlie," I said, holding out the money. "Keep the change."

But it wasn't Charlie. It was Pete.

And before I knew it, he hauled off and slugged me. I dropped to the floor like a sack of marbles.

Pete loomed over me, fuming, his hands still bunched into fists. "That's for even *thinking* about calling me Taki," he growled. He turned to leave, but then he stopped. "Oh, and I found out that you forged your pop's signature for the contest. If you have the guts to show your face at the ballpark on Saturday, I'm gonna tell your pop—and every-body else—that you're a rotten, cheating, no-good liar."

And then he stomped down the porch steps and out into the night.

CHAPTER

37

$\mathcal{T}$HERE I WAS, sprawled in the open doorway. The screen door drifted shut and bumped me on the head.

My left eye was throbbing, and it was already hard to see out of it. But all I could think of was the person who ratted me out.

"Ace!" How else could Pete know about me forging Pop's signature, unless someone told him? And the only person who knew about it, besides me, was Ace.

I crawled around, hunting for the spilled money with my one good eye. I managed to grab the dollar bill before it fluttered off the porch, and the quarters had rolled into a corner.

"Nicky?" called Ma from the kitchen. "What takes you so long?"

"Nothing, Ma!" I hollered back. I couldn't let her see my eye.

But then she was standing there, watching me crawl around on my hands and knees. I hadn't even heard her coming.

"Nicky! What happens to you?"

"Nothing, Ma," I told her, hauling myself to my feet. "I dropped the paperboy money."

She gave me a funny look and pushed past me onto the porch. She leaned out and scanned the sidewalk in both directions.

"I see somebody walking away," she said. She narrowed her eyes. "That is not the paper delivery boy."

"No, Ma," I said, turning my head so she couldn't see my face. "It wasn't the paperboy."

"Let me see you." She shut the door, grabbed my head, and inspected my face. But she didn't scream or anything. She just nodded and said, "Come with me." She pulled me behind her into the kitchen and sat me down at the table.

Lucky for me, Pop was still reading the newspaper and didn't bother to look up. "See this, Athena?" he said, as if she'd never left the room. "Here is a couple up in Cedarburg, they have been married for sixty-five years. How about that? They have their picture in the paper! Maybe someday you and I, we'll be in the newspaper. For getting old!" He chuckled at his own joke.

"That would be very nice," said Ma, but she wasn't really paying attention. She had the fridge open and was digging in the freezer compartment. Finally she pulled out a football-sized package wrapped in white butcher paper. "Fancy electric icebox has no ice," she muttered. "Take this." She unwrapped the package and handed me a rock-hard, black lump of something.

"It's not an icebox, Ma, it's a refrigerator-freezer," I said, taking the frozen lump. "It's electric. It doesn't need ice." She already knew all that, but as I might have mentioned before: My family loves having something to argue about. "What is this thing, anyway?" I held up the frozen hunk.

She leaned closer and inspected it with a sniff. "Liver." She pushed it against my eye. It was disgusting, but it did make my eye feel better.

"Did you pay the paperboy?" asked Pop, still behind his newspaper.

"Nope," I said, glancing up at Ma with my one good eye. "It, uh, wasn't the paperboy."

"Who was it?" Pop finally lowered the paper, and then he got a look at my face. "What happens to your eye?"

Before I could think up something to say, Ma actually stepped on my foot. "He slipped and fell down," she said to Pop. "It's just a bump. What else happens in the newspaper today?"

CHAPTER

38

AFTER ABOUT TEN MINUTES, the swelling around my eye had gone down and the liver was starting to get soft. I handed the slimy hunk of meat to Ma and wiped liver juice off my face with a towel.

"Let me see," she said, inspecting my eye. I guess she was satisfied with what she saw, because she rewrapped the liver and stuck it back in the freezer. "You are going to have a shiny eye tomorrow," she told me.

"A shiner," I told her. "Yeah, I guess." That Pete sure did have a lot of nerve.

And so did Ace.

"Say, Ma? I need to go over and see Ace for a minute, okay?"

She nodded. "Put on your jacket, *neh*?"

"Sure thing, Ma," I said, even though it was late May now and pretty warm outside. But I owed her.

Next door, I leaned on the bell. Ace answered the door, and I yanked him outside by his good arm.

"What's the deal?" he said.

"You ratted me out!"

"What?" Ace said. "I'd never—" And then he saw my face. "Holy smokes, what happened to your eye?"

"Pete punched me, that's what happened! He knows I forged my pop's signature on the batboy contest permission slip. How does he know that, Ace? You're the only other person who knew."

His ears went bright red. And then in a small voice he said, "Oops."

"What do ya mean, 'oops'?" I said.

"I didn't mean to do it!" he said. "We were out on the playground today, and he was bragging, ya know, how he always does. 'How did Nick even show up last Saturday?' Pete says, 'I thought that goody-two-shoes had to work Saturdays at his pop's dumb hat shop.' And I says to him, I says, 'Well, maybe you're not the only one who knows how to forge a parent's signature,' and then . . . I guess he figured it out."

"Ya think?"

"He egged me on!" said Ace in his own defense. "What was I supposed to do? Just stand there and let him call you goody-two-shoes and stuff?"

"You didn't have to spill all the beans!" I said. "Pete's been looking for an excuse to punch my lights out ever since I threatened to call him Taki." I dropped my voice at that last word, and glanced out toward the sidewalk. For all I knew, Pete was lurking in the shadows, waiting to strike again.

"Let me in." I pushed past Ace into his hallway.

He closed the door behind me. "When did you do that? And what's a Taki, anyway?"

"It's Pete's baby name. Remember that night when I hollered at him in Greek from your bedroom window?"

"Ohh," said Ace. "Taki? No wonder he's sore. That's even worse than Horace."

"Yeah, well, now I'm in big trouble," I told him. "My folks still don't know I lied about last Saturday. And just now they told me I could go to the game, and the parade, and everything! Pop gave me the whole day off, and I didn't even have to ask."

"That's great!" said Ace.

"Yeah, till Pete paid me a visit. In addition to leaving his calling card on my face, he dared me to show up on Saturday. He said that if I do, he'll tell everyone that I'm a liar. All because *you* couldn't keep your big mouth shut."

Ace sputtered. "Well . . . well, I wouldn't have to open *my* big mouth, sticking up for *you*, if Pete wasn't such a knucklehead!"

I gave him the stink-eye, so he tried again. "You just said Pete's been looking for an excuse to punch you. Which means he would've done it even if I hadn't spilled the beans about the forged signature."

He had a point. But I was still mad. "You owe me," I told him.

"Sure thing," he said, bouncing around me like a puppy. "Anything, just name it! But what're ya gonna do now? You deserve to be in that contest! And remember what he did to Penny. And the monkeys! You can't miss the monkeys."

"I'm not gonna miss anything," I told him. "What can Pop do to me after the fact? Well, okay, he can do a lot, but it'd be worth it. Besides, I'm not gonna let Pete push me around."

"That's the ticket!" said Ace, slapping me on the back with his good arm. "I'm behind you a hundred percent."

"Gee, thanks," I said. "But do me a favor? From now on, keep your mouth a hundred percent shut."

I spent all of the next day being sore at Ace. I avoided him at school, and even walked home by myself. Which was boring, and no fun, and way too quiet. I finally decided that having a bigmouth for a best friend was better than not having a best friend. And if I used all my energy being sore at Ace, I wouldn't have enough left over for hating Pete's guts, which I really needed in order to beat him on Saturday. So that night after supper, I went over to Ace's house and sat on his front porch until he noticed me. Then he came outside and sat down too. We both sat there, saying nothing, until it got dark.

"Tomorrow's the day," said Ace, finally.

"Yep," I said.

"Meet you out on the sidewalk first thing?"

"Yep."

And we both went inside, feeling a whole lot better.

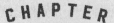

*A*ND THEN, IT WAS SATURDAY. The big day.

Me and Ace got up early and headed to the zoo. The morning newspaper had said that the caravan would be made up of four wagons, carrying two giraffes, a zebra, a rhinoceros (Tank!), and an unspecified number of monkeys.

"That way no one will get in trouble if any monkeys escape and are unaccounted for," said Ace.

"Or maybe it's just too much trouble trying to count a bunch of crazy monkeys," I told him.

"Suit yourself," he said. "But tonight I'm sleeping with my bedroom window open, just in case."

We found Penny at the zoo entrance on Frederick Street,

where the parade was supposed to start. "Nice shiner," she said when we walked up. "What happened?"

"It's a long story," I told her. "But keep an eye out for Pete, just in case. Here they come!"

Four army-green Parks Department trucks were lining up just inside the zoo entrance. Each truck was pulling a flatbed wagon fitted with a big metal cage. The cages were all decorated with buntings and flags, and each truck had a banner on its side that said what kind of animal was in the wagon behind it.

"Isn't it pretty obvious?" said Ace, reading a banner that said GIRAFFES.

He had a good point, but I told him, "It's all for show."

Behind the giraffes were the wagons with the zebra, the monkeys, and good ol' Tank. On the side of his truck was a yellow banner with black letters that said:

DANGER!
AFRICAN HOOK-LIPPED RHINOCEROS
2,580 POUNDS
KEEP CLEAR

And there was Tank, calm as could be, as if riding around the city streets and going to a ball game was something he did every day.

"Would you look at that," I said. "Tank can be a real cupcake sometimes."

"Yeah," said Penny. "A cupcake who almost took Ace's arm off." She looked down at Ace's smelly cast.

"It wasn't Tank's fault," said Ace. "My foot got caught on the fence."

"On the *rhinoceros* fence," Penny reminded him, "which you hopped over because you were being chased by a *rhinoceros*."

"I had to get our ball back," said Ace, very sensibly. "Look! A police escort!"

Sure enough, here came a squad car and four big Harleys, all with their lights spinning. They took their positions at the front of the caravan. Behind them, a marching band got into formation and started tuning up.

Next came the animal wagons. Bringing up the rear was an open-topped Jeep full of zookeepers in safari hats. One of the zookeepers even carried a huge gun.

"That's just for tranquilizers," I told Ace.

"I bet it's not," he said.

"Let's hope we don't find out," said Penny.

A big crowd of kids, and grown-ups, too, gathered behind the Jeep, ready to follow the whole procession to the ballpark. The sidewalks on both sides of Frederick Street were filling up with spectators, and police barricades kept the street clear of traffic.

And then, somewhere at the front of the line, a whistle blew—one long blast and four short ones. A bass drum picked up the beat, and then the snare drums busted out in a marching rhythm. Trumpets blared. Cymbals crashed. Monkeys screamed. And the caravan was on its way.

"Jeepers," I said. "I wish Ma and Pop were here to see this!"

CHAPTER

40

$\mathcal{L}$ ET ME TELL YOU, that parade was a sight to behold. Me and Ace and Penny joined the crowd of kids following behind the Jeep at the end of the caravan. All the way down Frederick Street to the Ol' Orchard, the band played, zoo wagons rumbled, kids followed, and spectators cheered.

The only part that wasn't perfect was when we marched past the Elegant Shoe Repair and Hat Shop. Pop was inside there somewhere, watching the celebration all alone. I pulled Ace and Penny to the near side of the street, so we could wave to him as we marched past, but I didn't know if he could see us. The big shop windows looked dark, almost as if the lights were turned off. But it was probably just the bright sunshine reflecting on the glass.

"Come on," said Ace, pulling me along to keep up with

the caravan. "Your pop said it was okay, remember? He wants you to have fun. So, have fun!"

He was right. I tried to focus on the music, and the flags, and the people waving. But I also kept an eye out for Pete. He was out there somewhere, and the last thing I needed was another ambush.

Before we knew it, we were at Orchard Field. The police escort led the whole procession straight into the ballpark through a big gate in left field, which was open just for the occasion. The zoo wagons and Jeep rumbled through behind the band, and all the people walking behind were corralled into a line by the ticket takers. Me and Ace had the bleacher tickets that we'd gotten for being in the batboy contest, and of course Penny had her ticket for Section One, Row One. Anyone without a ticket was herded toward the ticket windows around the home plate side of the stadium. It was crowded and confusing, and I bet that more than a few kids managed to sneak in for free. But I didn't think Joe Daggett would mind, at least not for today.

"Look!" said Penny as we followed the caravan through the gates and onto the outfield grass. "The radio announcers!"

Sure enough, two fellas were sitting on a platform out in the center-field bleachers, with their big radio microphones set up on a table in front of them. They were wearing head-phones over their Mudpuppies baseball caps, and they were holding big paper cups. The stands were filling up with fans too, and a big banner on the center-field fence read **RESERVED FOR BATBOY CONTESTANTS**.

"Looks like it's going to be a full house," I said.

The whole caravan paraded one full circuit around the field, starting in left field, marching down the foul line past third base, around behind home plate, and then out to right field along the first-base line. The crowd gathering in the stands cheered as the caravan went past.

The marching band finished playing "The Stars and Stripes Forever," and the caravan came to a halt in center field. Then we heard a loud scratching noise as the loudspeakers crackled to life.

"Ladies and gentlemen! Boys and girls!"

"It's Joe Daggett!" I said. There he was, standing at home plate with his big microphone.

"Welcome to the first annual combined celebration of Mudpuppies baseball and the Zoo Spring Opening!"

The crowd cheered and stomped their feet. All around the ballpark, the wooden stands rumbled like thunder.

Joe Daggett waited for the cheering to quiet down, and then he continued. "May I present today's live radio announcers! You know them as the hosts of the ever-popular *Top o' the Morning* program, every weekday from six to nine on WTRJ. Give a warm welcome to our very own Ray Hinkley and Bob Gillespie!"

More cheers, and from their platform in the center-field bleachers, the two announcers held up their paper cups and waved to the fans.

"Take it away, Ray and Bob!" said Joe Daggett.

The loudspeakers crackled again, and then there was dead silence. Everybody looked around, wondering what happened, but then the speakers boomed to life.

CHAPTER

41

Transcript of live radio broadcast of
May 29, 1948

BOB:
—the heck is wrong with this thing?
Hey! There we go! Howdy, folks,
it's your old pals Ray and Bob here,
broadcasting live from Orchard Field
on this very special occasion!

RAY:
That's right, Bob! What a beautiful
day here at the Ol' Orchard! Thanks
to the Mudpuppies for hosting

us, and to our sponsor for today,
Doerflinger's Artificial Limb
Company.

BOB:
Doerflinger's. Your source for
corsets, braces, crutches, and
all your orthopedic needs. Call
Doerflinger's today at MArquette
0114!

RAY:
For you folks listening at home,
this is a sight to behold. Imagine
a whole caravan of wild beasts,
right there in the outfield! They're
parading around the warning track as
we speak.

BOB:
I've never seen such a spectacle,
Ray. The whole procession is being
led by our city's finest men in
blue. Four motorcycles and a prowler
car. Right behind them we have the
Riverwest High School Marching Band.

RAY:

Don't they sound swell, Bob?

BOB:

They're in great form today, Ray. Here come the zoo wagons now! They sure do look spiffy, don't they? What would you call those, Ray? Circus wagons? Rolling cages?

RAY:

I guess you'd call 'em one of a kind, Bob!

BOB:

Ain't that the truth, Ray! First up, we have the sweetest pair of giraffes you ever did see. A mother and baby, I'm guessing. Would you look at that, Ray? The top of the cage is open! What a majestic— Whoops! The mama giraffe just reached out and plucked a baseball cap right off the head of a lad in the front row of the bleachers! Don't you worry, buddy. I'm sure

you'll get your cap back, as soon
as Mrs. Giraffe finds out it doesn't
fit, ha ha!

RAY:
I hope that kid doesn't mind giraffe
slobber, Bob. It looks pretty soggy,
even from up here.

BOB:
Quite a souvenir that would be! Next
we have— What's that in the next
wagon, Ray?

RAY:
There's a banner on the side of the
truck, Bob. It's monkeys! A wagonload
of screeching, skittering, screaming
monkeys!

BOB:
How many monkeys do you suppose are
in that cage, Ray?

RAY:
No one knows, Bob. They won't hold

still *long enough for anyone to count.*

BOB:
Those monkeys sure are a hit with the crowd, aren't they, Ray? Listen to that applause.

RAY:
Good thing there's bars across the top of the monkey cage, Bob. No grabbing baseball caps for these fellas. Can you imagine those monkeys getting out and swarming all over the field?

BOB:
It's fun to imagine, that's for sure, Ray. Hey, kids, better sleep with your windows open tonight, just in case! Who wouldn't want a pet monkey? Here comes the next wagon, Ray. Look at that horse in striped pajamas, ha ha!

RAY:
Don't worry, folks. It's a zebra. He sure is regal looking, isn't he? Say,

Bob, have you seen that refreshment
vendor around anyplace? I'm parched.

BOB:
I just called him over, Ray. That
zebra is a beautiful animal, to be
sure. Now, ladies and gentlemen,
here comes the last wagon. What kind
of animal is that, I wonder? An
elephant? No—a hippo?

RAY:
The banner on the side of the truck,
Bob. The banner.

BOB:
Oh, I see it there, thanks, Ray! It's
a very dangerous-looking African
hook-lipped rhinoceros, the banner
says. Weighs 2,580 pounds!

RAY:
Whoa, Nellie, that fella sure is
big! Now, ladies and gentlemen,
bringing up the rear of the caravan
is an army-surplus Jeep, occupied by

several esteemed members of our local
Zoological Society.

BOB:
Is that an elephant gun that zookeeper
is carrying in the back of that Jeep?

RAY:
I'm sure it's just for tranquilizers,
Bob.

BOB:
If you say so, Ray. That rhinoceros
sure is a strong-looking fella!

RAY:
Well, folks, that wraps up our
cavalcade of zoo animals. Aren't
they a swell bunch of specimens,
Bob? But the fans in the stands
can still get a good look at them,
because the wagons will stay right
out there in center field for the
duration of the pregame festivities.
What's coming up next, Bob?

BOB:

Well, Ray, I'm told we have a very special surprise guest throwing out the first pitch! But first, it's time to choose the batboy for today's game.

RAY:

That's right, Bob. Which of six lucky finalists will win the title of Mudpuppy for a Day? Stay tuned, after this message of interest from Doerflinger's!

*T*HAT ZOO CARAVAN WAS THE BEST. About a zillion kids (including me and Ace and Penny) got to stay on the field and follow the procession around. Then the police escort zoomed off the field, sirens blaring, and Joe Daggett appeared at home plate again to make another announcement.

"Ladies and gentlemen! Boys and girls! It's time to commence the final competition for Mudpuppy for a Day!"

"This is it!" said Ace, slapping my back with his good arm. "Go out there and show that Pete who's boss!"

All of a sudden my hands felt sweaty, and my black eye throbbed. Joe Daggett still hadn't announced the details of the final contest. Would it be hitting? Fielding? Would Pete slug me again, in front of all these people?

"Don't worry," said Penny, as if she knew exactly what I was thinking. "You're ready."

Then Joe Daggett invited the six finalists to join him at home plate, and everybody else to get off the field. So all the kids scattered, mostly in the direction of the outfield bleachers, behind the banner that read **RESERVED FOR BATBOY CONTESTANTS**.

"Hey, Ace," said Penny, holding him back. "Do you want to sit with me behind home plate until Josie gets here?"

Ace practically leapt out of his skin. "Gee, thanks, Penny!"

I'm telling ya, that Penny is a swell girl.

So we all hurried toward home plate, where the other finalists were already gathering, including Pete. "Hiya, Mr. Daggett!" said Ace real loud as he and Penny sauntered past on their way to the grandstand. Ace made sure Pete was watching as an usher opened a gate in the backstop, and he and Penny sat down, front and center.

Pete stood there staring, and I could tell he was starting to fume. Then he noticed me.

"You sure have a lot of nerve showing your face here, Spirakis," he growled as I walked up to the group. "Wait'll I tell your pop."

I turned and faced him with my nose just inches from his. "My pop knows I'm here," I told him. And then I pointed to my black eye. "See this shiner, Pete? This is nothing compared to what I'm gonna do to you today, right here in front of all these people."

I had no idea what I meant by that, but sure as shootin' I wasn't gonna let Pete get the last word.

Joe Daggett did his best to herd all six of us together. "Ladies and gentlemen!" he announced into the microphone. "May I present our six Mudpuppy for a Day finalists! These bright young fellas were the finalists in a special competition here at Orchard Field last Saturday."

Then he announced us by name, one at a time. Each kid stepped forward and accepted a brand-new Mudpuppies ball cap from Joe Daggett. The crowd applauded politely while they waited for the good stuff. I couldn't blame them. When Joe Daggett read off Pete's name, Pete swaggered around in a circle, waving his cap like he was Babe Ruth at Yankee Stadium. I wanted to slug him.

"Last but not least . . . ," announced Joe Daggett, winking at me. But when he looked at the piece of paper in his hand, he stopped and scratched his head. He looked at me, and then at the paper, and then at me again. "Mick Sparks?"

I hopped over to where he was standing, and he put his hand over the microphone. "Nick Spirakis," I said in his ear.

"That's it!" said Joe Daggett. Then he took his hand off the microphone and said real loud, "Nick Spirakis, everyone! Let's give our finalists a big round of applause!"

The crowd clapped politely again, but they weren't really paying attention. Would you? When there was still a wagonload of monkeys in center field?

"I suppose you fellas are wondering what the final contest is gonna be," said Joe Daggett into the microphone as he looked us over. "Any guesses?"

We all stood there in a line, with our mouths hanging open for a second, and then we launched into suggestions. For all we knew, Joe Daggett would pick the one he liked the best.

"Batting," said Pete, sticking out his chest. I hate that Pete.

"Base-running!" hollered this kid who was even smaller than Ace. But he could probably run really fast.

The other fellas started yelling stuff too, and even the crowd in the stands hollered suggestions. Pitching. Giving signs, reading signs. Stealing signs. Stealing bases. Fielding.

Oh, jeepers, not fielding!

"Okay, okay," said Joe Daggett, laughing and holding up a hand. "Those are all dandy suggestions. But if you ask me, there's one skill a batboy needs more than any other, and that's the ability to pay attention. When you're standing out there in foul territory, you'd better be on your toes, watching for foul balls, signals from the umpire. Monkeys on the field. Ha! I made that last one up!"

That got the biggest cheer of the day so far.

Joe Daggett waited for the cheering to die down, and then he looked at the six of us. "Okay, fellas, are you ready?"

We all leaped in the air and cheered.

But my heart was pounding. My hands were clammy. Please please please don't make me have to catch a fly ball.

Joe Daggett held on to the microphone with both hands. "The contest is one simple question," he said. He paused for dramatic effect. "Our first annual Mudpuppy for a Day will be the one of you who comes closest to telling me the correct weight of that rhinoceros out there in right field."

CHAPTER 43

*I*ALMOST COULDN'T BELIEVE my ears when Joe Daggett announced the final contest question. A couple of the other guys said they remembered seeing Tank's weight printed on the banner, but now the banner was gone, and neither of them could remember the right number.

Pete just stood there with his hands balled into fists. He was so mad that puffs of smoke started coming out of his ears. (I might be making up that last part. But everything else is true, I swear.)

So it was even more fun than it should've been to march right up to Joe Daggett, grab the microphone, and announce loud and clear, "That rhinoceros out there in right field weighs exactly 2,580 pounds. Oh, and his name is Tank."

Joe Daggett's mouth dropped open, and then he broke into a huge grin. "Ladies and gentlemen!" he said, after he pried the microphone out of my hands. "Today's winner—guessing the rhino's weight *exactly*—and our first official Mudpuppy for a Day: Nick Spirakis!"

The crowd went wild, and I swear that from their seats behind home plate, Ace and Penny were cheering the loudest.

Joe Daggett shook my hand and slapped me on the back. "Head on into the locker room, Nick, and put on that Mudpuppies uniform!"

And I escaped down the steps of the dugout and into the locker room before Pete could pulverize me.

Miss Garble was waiting for me with my glove and a brand-new uniform, number 00. She handed me the gear and then scurried out of the room so she wouldn't see me in my underwear.

Once I was dressed, I looked at myself in a mirror.

The uniform was too big for me, but I don't mind telling you: I looked pretty darn good.

I grabbed my mitt and headed up to the dugout and onto the field, just like a real ballplayer.

BOB:
Here he comes out of the dugout, Ray!

*Doesn't the lad look sharp in his
Pups uniform!*

RAY:
*Our winner, for those of you
listening at home, is . . . let's
see my notes here . . . twelve-year-
old Mick Sparks! Congrats to Mick,
and to all the fellas who did their
darnedest to win this competition!*

BOB:
*Mick sure earned it, Ray. That kid
marched right up and gave the rhino's
correct weight, as if he knew that
rhinoceros personally!*

RAY:
*Right on the nose, Bob. Or should I
say horn, ha ha. Now the teams are
lining up on the baselines. Listen
to those cheers! If I didn't know
better, I'd say the atmosphere here
in the ballpark was more like the
World Series than a Saturday in May.*

BOB:

We should be so lucky, Ray.
Say, Ray, is that rhino wagon
supposed to be rocking like that?

RAY:

How's that, Bob? Oh, I see. Sure
enough, folks, the rhinoceros appears
to be getting a bit feisty out there
in right field. I guess he wants the
game to start too, ha ha.

BOB:

Wow, look at that wagon sway! If I
didn't know better, I'd say that
critter is liable to bust out!

RAY:

I'm sure the zookeepers have taken
all the necessary precautions,
Bob. Uh-oh. I don't think that was
supposed to happen.

BOB:

We have a breach! We have a breach!

RAY:

Calm down, Bob. Well, folks, it seems the rhino has found a weakness in his wagon. . . .

BOB:

Weakness?? He just busted out!

RAY:

Ladies and gentlemen, you're not gonna believe this, but we seem to have a rhinoceros on the loose in the outfield. I think it's safe to say we'll have an official delay of game. I bet you can't find this anywhere in the official rule book, ha ha.

BOB:

Run, you people, run!

RAY:

The players are making a break for it! Most of them have hightailed it back to the dugout, but a handful are sprinting for the bull pen.

That's ironic, isn't it, Bob? Maybe we should start calling it the rhino pen, ha ha!

BOB:
Watch out! Holy cow, did you see that, Ray?

RAY:
That's definitely what I'd call a near miss, Bob. Thank goodness that umpire was fast on his feet. Well, folks, it appears that everyone is off the field and out of danger.

BOB:
Wait! Do you see what I see, Ray?

RAY:
I'm afraid I do, Bob. It seems the rhinoceros has fixed his beady eye on that group of ballplayers in the bull pen. Which is unfortunate, because there's nothing between them and the rhino except fifty feet

of *beautifully manicured outfield grass.*

BOB:
Uh-oh. He's heading in the direction of the bull pen! I thought rhinos had bad eyesight!

RAY:
Very bad eyesight, according to my notes here. Very good hearing, apparently. Who knew? With those tiny ears?

BOB:
The players are trapped in the bull pen! There's no escape! If they run for it, the rhino will mow them down like . . . like . . .

RAY:
It won't be pretty, Bob. Let's just leave it at that.

BOB:
Hold your horses, Ray! One player

just ran back out onto the field!
Who's number zero zero, Ray?

RAY:

Holy smokes, Bob, that's the batboy!
Now he's just standing there, all
alone in center field. He's actually
waving his arms and yelling. If
I didn't know better, I'd say he
was trying to attract the rhino's
attention!

BOB:

It's working! The rhino is turning
away from the bull pen and toward the
batboy! The players are taking this
chance to hightail it down the first-
base line and into the safety of the
dugout.

RAY:

The rhino sees the batboy, all right.
Now it's lowering its massive head.
That can't be good. Uh-oh! I can't
look!

What was I supposed to do? There was Tank, free as a bird (a fat, leathery, stumpy-legged bird), and all those ballplayers in the bull pen were sitting ducks (tall, skinny, sitting ducks).

So I ran out to center field. I hopped around and hollered, and pretty soon Tank noticed me. I waved at the fellas in the bull pen to get out of there. Most of them ran for the dugout, but a few of them hopped the railing and into the stands along the first-base line.

But Tank wasn't paying attention to them anymore.

He was paying attention to me.

The crowd in the bleachers hollered their encouragement.

"What're ya doing, kid?"

"I think he's crazy, that's what I think!"

And then, slicing through all the noise like a worm through dirt, came a familiar voice. Its owner was in the front row of the bleachers, leaning out over the center-field fence.

"Some batboy you are!" hollered Pete. "What, are ya scared of a little ol' rhino?"

I dropped my mitt and sized up the situation: I could tear across the grass and hop the right-field fence to safety. Six seconds, tops.

Or never. Depending on the reflexes of the rhino.

Tank ran toward me.

I ran faster.

It was just like old times. And this time, I didn't even tear my pants.

BOB:
Holy smokes! I didn't know rhinos could run that fast!

RAY:
Thank goodness that batboy was faster, Bob. Did you see how he sprinted across the grass and vaulted over the right-field fence? It's like he's done it before.

BOB:
Is that a rhino-shaped dent in the right-field fence, Ray?

RAY:
That might be a bit of an exaggeration, Bob.

BOB:
Not by much, folks! That was a close one!

RAY:

How do ya like that, Bob? That rhino has gone right back to eating the grass again. It's like someone turned off a switch.

BOB:

That's right, folks. Now that everybody's off the field, the rhino has calmed down considerably and has started grazing the outfield.

RAY:

Say, Bob, maybe the Mudpuppies can fire their grounds crew now, ha ha.

BOB:

What's he doing now?

RAY:

It looks like he's headed back toward his wagon, Bob. I wouldn't believe it if I wasn't seeing it with my own eyes.

BOB:

Sure enough, Ray. Apparently, during all the commotion, the zookeeper finally woke up—I mean, had the presence of mind to open the door of the cage and deploy the ramp. Now he appears to be coaxing the rhino up the ramp with . . . what is that, Ray? Is that the elephant gun? No, wait. It's a celery stalk.

RAY:

And just like that, the rhino is safely back in his cage. I hope the latch holds this time, ha ha! I wouldn't believe it if I hadn't seen with my own eyes, folks. Right here at the Ol' Orchard: a rhino in right field.

BOB:

Well, Ray, after all that excitement, there's only one thing left to say.

RAY:

What's that, Bob?

BOB:

Play ball!

CHAPTER

44

*T*HAT'S RIGHT. Not only did I win Mudpuppy for a Day, but I saved half the Mudpuppies starting lineup (and most of the pitching staff) from Tank.

After it was all over, and everyone was safe, the whole ballpark hollered and stomped and waved pennants. The marching band up in the bleachers launched into "For He's a Jolly Good Fellow" and I got to run out onto the field and wave my cap.

After all that, everybody practically forgot there was a ball game to be played. But the Parks Department trucks started their engines, and the zoo wagons finally rolled out of the ballpark through the left-field fence. Not a single monkey had gotten loose, which probably disappointed Ace, but personally, I don't think I could've taken any more excitement.

From the bleachers, the marching band played "Yankee Doodle Dandy" as the wagons rolled out. Out in the street, the police escort fired up their lights and sirens, and off went the whole procession, back to the zoo for more speeches and presentations.

I peeked out of the dugout to give the thumbs-up to Penny and Ace. They were having a swell time, with cotton candy and bags of peanuts.

The manager showed me around the dugout and explained my batboy duties. "Stand here at the top of the dugout steps, and keep your eye on the umpire. If he signals for fresh baseballs, be ready to hustle out there and hand over a few. And keep your eye on the ball. Always wear your glove, and be ready for those hard-lining foul balls. They can take your head right off. If any of our players actually manages to reach base, it's your job to run out and grab the bat off home plate and bring it back to the dugout. Got all that?"

"Sure thing, skip," I said, trying not to think how I was supposed to keep my eye on all that stuff at the same time. "For the visiting team too?"

"Heck, no," said the manager. "I hope they trip and break their necks." He nudged me and winked. "Don't worry, kid. That's what you call home field advantage. And keep the water jugs filled, and make sure there's plenty of sunflower seeds. Piece of cake!" He slapped me on the back, and then he moseyed over to hand his lineup card to the umpire. The players were taking warm-up swings or rubbing spit into their gloves. And Joe Daggett was over at the backstop, leaning on his cane and talking to Ace and Penny. It was still about ten minutes until first pitch, so I went over to see what was up.

"Your sister should be here any minute now," Joe Daggett was saying to Penny. He checked his watch. "Her train was scheduled to arrive twenty minutes ago. I sent someone down to the station to pick her up."

Just then, one of the Pups players jogged out from the dugout.

"Mr. Daggett? Phone call for you."

"Oh, good," said Joe Daggett. "I'll bet that's Bill. I told him to call me on the dugout phone when the train got in." Joe Daggett limped over to the dugout, and I followed him. Because I was the batboy, and I was allowed.

Joe Daggett picked up the telephone receiver from where it rested on the shelf. "Hello, Bill? How goes it? Did you find our shortstop?"

A voice buzzed through the phone. With all the ballpark noise, I couldn't make out any of the words, but the person on the other end was talking really fast.

"What's that?" said Joe Daggett. "Slow down, Bill. Say that again?" He plugged his other ear with a finger so he could hear better.

Then Joe Daggett yelped. "Late?! How late? A whole hour? How on earth—what do you mean, traffic jam? How the heck can there be a traffic jam? It's a train!"

The voice on the other end of the line said something else.

Joe Daggett's eyebrows popped up. "You don't say. A cow? On the tracks? Wait a minute: Doesn't the train have one of those cowcatcher things on the front? I thought trains had cowcatcher things."

Bill's voice again.

"You don't say," said Joe Daggett. "No, Bill, of course nobody wants to hurt the cow! Okay. Keep me posted. Get here as quick as you can, all right?" And he hung up the phone with a *klunk*.

"Miss Garble!"

Miss Garble appeared out of nowhere with a clipboard in her arms. "Yes, Mr. Daggett?"

"We've run into a snag. Our All-American Girl baseball player won't be here in time to throw out the first pitch. She's somewhere on the godforsaken prairie, stuck behind a Jersey cow."

"Are you sure?" said Miss Garble.

"That's what Bill just told me, Miss Garble!" said Joe Daggett.

"I mean, are you sure it's a Jersey? It's just that I grew up on a dairy farm, Mr. Daggett, and most cows around here are Holsteins. Is it a brown cow, or black and white?"

227

"How do I know what color it is?" said Joe Daggett.

"Because if it's black and white, it's definitely a Holstein."

"Miss Garble, unless you can drive down there and coax that cow off the tracks before game time, I don't really want a lesson on dairy farming right now."

"Yes, Mr. Daggett," said Miss Garble. "What'll we do now?"

"That's a very good question," said Joe Daggett. "Do you see all those people out there in the stands, Miss Garble? I promised them that a girl baseball player would throw out the first pitch, and I'm not about to disappoint them. So either you need to suit up and grab a mitt, or we'd better think of something else, toot sweet."

That's when I stepped forward.

"Mr. Daggett?" I said. "Can I make a suggestion?"

CHAPTER

45

*A*ND THAT'S HOW PENNY got to throw out the first pitch at an official Mudpuppies baseball game, in front of a standing-room-only crowd.

I dragged Joe Daggett out of the dugout and over to where Penny was sitting, and explained the situation to her (except I skipped the part about Jersey versus Holstein cows, which I think Mr. Daggett really appreciated). So Penny told Joe Daggett how she practiced with her sister all the time, including overhand pitching. Me and Ace told Joe Daggett how Penny had a rocket-launcher for an arm. And it was settled.

And there she was a few minutes later: on the mound, in front of ten thousand people, with her hair jammed up under a brand-new, official Mudpuppies baseball cap. She hitched up her Rosie the Riveter overalls, dug in with a saddle shoe, and fired that ball clear across home plate, right into the catcher's mitt, without even one bounce. She threw so hard that her cap popped right off, and her crazy mop of hair busted out in a big cloud all around her head.

Maybe it was the overalls, but when Joe Daggett announced to the crowd that Penny Lonergan would throw out the first pitch, they sounded a little disappointed. Or maybe it was because they'd been promised a real professional player for the Kenosha Comets, and now she was stuck behind a cow. Or maybe they didn't really believe they were watching a girl. When there are pro ballplayers named Christy and Babe and stuff, who could blame them? But when that cap popped off Penny's head, and everybody got a load of her hair, and finally realized that they'd just seen a rocket of a pitch thrown by a twelve-year-old *girl*, the crowd went wild.

Practically the entire Mudpuppies team busted out of the dugout, lifted Penny onto their shoulders, and carried her to her seat behind home plate. I don't know if that's what Penny had in mind when she'd told Joe Daggett that girls could do stuff, but it was pretty swell.

And then something really strange happened.

As I was going back to the dugout to get a supply of baseballs for the start of the game, I saw something—or should I say, some*one*—in the stands, about ten rows behind the Pups dugout.

"Pop?"

It was hard to see his face, because he was wearing a fedora—everyone was wearing fedoras, of course—but I stared pretty hard, and he stared hard at me too, and then his caterpillar eyebrows shot up behind his glasses, and he pulled his fedora down over his face and slumped down in his seat.

That sealed the deal. It had to be him. You don't pull your hat down over your face and slump down in your seat if you *want* to be spotted.

"How do ya like that?" I said to myself. "Pop's playing hooky." All that talk at the dinner table the other night, about how baseball games are for kids, and not for successful businessmen with responsibilities. And now here he was, at the game. And I bet he hadn't told Ma, or anyone else, because why else would he be slumping down in his seat?

I thought about the dark windows of the Elegant Shoe Repair and Hat Shop as we'd paraded past earlier in the day. Had Pop already closed up shop by then? Or did he watch the parade going by and think, *Aw, heck. I can't miss this! Look at all those monkeys!*

It didn't really matter. Pop was here. At the game.

Which also meant he'd caught me in a lie. Because, even

though I had permission to be at the game, there was only one way I could be hanging around the Mudpuppies dugout, in a Mudpuppies uniform, and he knew it.

But at least for now, he couldn't say anything. Because I'd caught *him* at something too.

I'd caught him having fun.

CHAPTER

46

*L*ET ME TELL YOU, being Mudpuppy for a Day is a lot of work. I barely had time to worry about whether or not I was in trouble.

There I was, in the dugout, or on the infield, for the entire game. I hauled jugs of water from the clubhouse up to the dugout, hustled supplies of muddy baseballs out to the umpire, and scrambled around collecting bats, rosin bags, and the occasional wad of bubblegum. Sure, I wasn't allowed outside foul territory, but it was still swell. The whole world looks different from the steps of a dugout.

The Pups were down 4–0 by the third inning, but to be honest, I really didn't care. And I stopped worrying about the visiting team tripping over their bats left at home plate. The Pups needed whatever home field advantage they could get.

It was 6–0 in the fourth when I noticed someone new sitting next to Penny. It must have been her sister, Josie, finally escaped from the clutches of the Holstein, or the Jersey, or whatever kind of cow had held her train hostage somewhere between here and Kenosha. She was wearing her Comets uniform, which looked swell except for a ridiculous-looking short skirt. I mean, you could see her knees! If you think it's embarrassing to miss a high fly ball in front of people, imagine what it must be like to play ball in that skirt. I just hoped she was wearing some kind of bloomers underneath.

But she looked happy, and Penny looked *really* happy, so it was all okay by me.

And somehow, Ace had managed to keep his seat on the other side of Penny. Good ol' Ace.

By the sixth inning, it was 10–0, but the stands were still full, because Joe Daggett had arranged surprise giveaways between every inning. If the number on your ticket stub matched the number that the radio announcers called, you won a free bag of popcorn, or cotton candy, or a soda. It's amazing how many people stuck around to see the Pups play a lousy game, just for the chance to march down and collect ten cents' worth of snacks in front of a whole crowd of people.

Then it was time for the seventh inning stretch. Out in the center-field bleachers, the marching band launched into a rendition of "Take Me Out to the Ball Game," so I had a chance to look around and take it all in. I scanned the grandstand for Pop, but I didn't see him. Maybe he'd left early, to get back to work before Ma stopped by the shop and found out that he was playing hooky.

Which was kind of funny, because now I saw, up there in the stands, with a bag of popcorn as big as her head, my very own mother.

I know what you're thinking: What are the chances that I'd spot first my pop, and then my ma, in a stadium packed with ten thousand people? All I can say is, more than once I've seen a baby monkey pick out its own mother from a zillion identical-looking possibilities scurrying around on Monkey Island. So maybe it's not so strange after all.

Plus, Ma was wearing her favorite hat with yellow flowers and waving at me like she was signaling the coast guard from a sinking ship.

She stood up from her seat and started down the steps toward the dugout, the little flowers on her hat bobbing.

I thought about pretending I didn't see her, but who was I kidding? I went over to meet her (and my fate) at the railing.

"Nicky!" Her cheeks were flushed and her popcorn was spilling out of the bag. "You won the big prize! I am very proud of you." And that dugout railing was the only thing that saved me from getting my cheek pinched in front of all those people.

"You saw that? Thanks, Ma." Maybe I didn't need to be so worried after all.

She offered me some popcorn. "But there is something I don't understand."

"What's that, Ma?"

"The announcer, he said that the boys in the contest were here last Saturday too." She squinted at me. "You did not go to the state capitol last Saturday?" It wasn't really a question.

"Not exactly, Ma."

She shook her head. The yellow flowers jiggled. "I will have to tell your father about this."

I had no idea what to say to that.

But that reminded me. "What are *you* doing here, Ma? Didn't you have a Ladies' Guild meeting at church today?"

She shrugged and offered me some more popcorn. "I went to the meeting, *neh*. But I only stay long enough to quit."

I almost fell over. "Ma! You quit the Ladies' Guild?"

She licked salt off her fingers. "And then I take the Number Thirty-Seven streetcar, and I come here."

"But, Ma, why did you quit? What about your *koulouria*?"

She waved a hand. "I don't need Mrs. Costas and the Ladies' Guild to tell me my *koulouria* are delicious. My family, they tell me. Plenty of other things I can do at the church, anyway. Maybe I can teach Greek school. The little ones—first, second grade. I could teach them to read and write in Greek, *neh*?"

"And they could help you learn to read English," I said. "That's a great idea, Ma!"

She inspected my black eye. "It was Taki Costas who punched you the other night, *neh*?"

"Yeah," I admitted. "Did you see him?"

"I guessed," she said. "Remember second grade? You hit Taki on the steps outside church. You made his nose bleed."

My face got warm. "You saw *that*?"

She nodded. "I was on the sidewalk, talking to Mrs. Costas. Taki tried to punch you first, but he missed. But Mrs. Costas, she only saw the next part. Ever since, she thinks my Nicky is a bully to her Taki. *Hmph!*"

"How come you never said anything before?"

She sighed. "I was looking the other way too, *neh*? I tell myself that Mrs. Costas, she is president of the Ladies' Guild. I must be nice to her. I let her tell me what's true, instead of believing my own eyes. But Mrs. Costas is a bully, just like her son. I have no more time for bullies."

"Aw, gee, Ma." I reached out, and—just because—I pinched her cheek. "And you came to the game."

She grinned. "Ladies' Day. Half price. But don't tell your father. The poor man, he works so hard. I know he wishes he could be here too."

"You don't know the half of it, Ma."

And of all the crazy things that happened at the ballpark that day, the craziest thing happened next.

Just as the marching band played the last notes of "Take Me Out to the Ball Game," with everyone singing along—"For it's ONE! TWO! Three strikes you're out, at the OLD! BALL! GAME!"—there was a big gasp, and then a cheer from the crowd. Because, out there at the front of the center-field bleachers, a brand-new banner had unfurled, covering the one reading **RESERVED FOR BATBOY CONTESTANTS**. The new banner said:

EAT AT SPARKY'S!
THE BEST CUSTARD IN TOWN!

CHAPTER 47

𝓕INALLY IT WAS THE BOTTOM OF THE NINTH, and I don't mind telling you I was glad, even though my day of fame was coming to an end. But I was worn out, and hungry, and it was 10–2, for crikey's sake, and the Pups needed to be put out of their misery.

The first two batters went down swinging, and the manager told me to start packing up. So I went out to gather up the donut weights and stray batting gloves from the on-deck circle.

But I hadn't noticed that the next batter was already at the plate, and the pitcher was winding up to throw.

"Hey, kid, you're not supposed to be out here," said the on-deck hitter, who looked like he was ready to go home too.

239

Before I could answer, I heard the crack of a bat. I flinched and—pure reflex—I raised my glove in front of my face. (I know. I was still wearing my glove. The manager had told me never to take it off, and I wanted to make a good impression.) Anyhow, I didn't get creamed by any screaming line drive, thank goodness. But I hadn't seen the pitch either, so I didn't get a good read on the ball. To be honest, I had no idea where it was.

Then I saw all the infielders staring up into the sky. The catcher leapt into a standing position, yanked off his mask, and tossed it to the side.

It was a high pop-up.

"Get out of the way, kid!" hollered someone in the stands, but by the time I realized he was hollering at *me*, it was too late. The catcher came running over toward the on-deck circle, his eyes still on the ball (which apparently was somewhere in the stratosphere), and his mind bent on getting the final out of the game. He didn't see me, or the on-deck batter, and the on-deck batter didn't see the catcher, because he was watching the ball too, and trying to figure out which way to run, like a squirrel in the middle of the street when a car is coming.

And then, a whole bunch of stuff happened really quickly. The catcher barreled into the on-deck batter, and they both fell onto the grass in a tangled heap. I managed to scoot out of the way just in time, but then I realized I still hadn't seen the ball.

I looked up. And here it came, screaming out of the sky like a comet out for revenge.

You might not believe me when I tell you that I had time to think how ironic this whole situation was. Here I stood, on the on-deck circle during the bottom of the ninth of an actual minor league baseball game, wearing a professional baseball uniform, on a real baseball field, with loads of people watching, and a high fly ball was coming right at me.

Okay, I didn't actually have time to think all that, at least not at that moment, which was a good thing, because if I *had* had a chance to actually think, I probably would've frozen up like I always do when I see a fly ball coming my way.

All I could do was raise my glove and hope for the best.

I heard a loud *thunk*.

I looked down and there was the ball, resting in my glove. *My* glove.

The crowd went wild.

Well, mostly they were laughing, but they were cheering for me too. I looked over to Penny, who was cheering so hard, she dropped a whole bag of popcorn. Her sister Josie was cheering too. Over in the Pups dugout, even the manager and the ballplayers gave me a round of applause.

Then somebody was hollering at me. "Hey, kid!" It was

the catcher, and he was hopping mad. "Get off the field! You made me miss the last out!"

"Sorry," I said. I tossed him the ball and started toward the dugout. But then I turned back to him and hollered, "That's what you call home field advantage!"

CHAPTER

48

*I*T TOOK JUST ONE MORE pitch for the game to end. The Pups lost, 10–2. But it didn't seem like anyone in that whole ballpark even cared. It had been a swell day all around.

I had to stay after the game and clean up the entire dug-out, which I did in a hurry, so I could get out of there in case Pop came looking for me. I hustled to sweep up paper cups and sunflower husks, keeping an eye out for Pop and his fedora. But he must have left, and I guess Ma did too, because I didn't see either one of them. Maybe they both figured they'd better hurry home before the other one found out that they'd been to the ball game when they were supposed to be doing other stuff.

And yet, ironically, *I* was the one in trouble.

"There he is!" said a voice from the other end of the empty dugout.

I looked up. "Hiya, Mr. Daggett!"

He hobbled over with his cane and sat down on the bench. "Well? How was it?"

"It was great," I told him. "My pop came to the game! And so did my ma."

"Did they? Well, good for them! I bet they're real proud of you."

I shifted my feet. "Something like that."

"Mr. Daggett?" said a voice behind me.

We both turned, and there was Miss Garble, appearing out of nowhere again. She would've made a great spy during the war.

"Yes, Miss Garble?"

"There are some . . . people here to see you." She stepped aside, and there was Ace and Penny, and Penny's sister Josie in her Kenosha Comets uniform with the skirt that was so short. She was tall like Penny, and had the same dark hair, but it was pinned up all neat under her ball cap. She was wearing lipstick, but just a little. It wasn't all smeared on, the way Sophie Costas wore it.

Ace lifted his arm as he squeezed past Miss Garble. "Wanna sign my cast?" It looked like it had been used to dredge a pond.

"No thank you," said Miss Garble, flattening herself

against the wall like he had malaria or something.

Josie shook Joe Daggett's hand and thanked him for inviting her, and apologized for being too late to throw out the first pitch.

"Don't give it another thought," said Joe Daggett. "We're glad you finally made it, and your sister here did a dandy job."

"So I hear," said Josie, beaming at Penny. "I'm sorry I missed that too."

"I bet we can arrange for both of you to do it again," said Joe Daggett. "I'm like *this* with the Pups' president." He held up two crossed fingers and winked at Ace.

"I taught him that," Ace whispered into my ear.

Joe Daggett turned to Josie. "Now you have to tell me, Miss Lonergan, because I'm dying to know: Was it a brown cow, or a black-and-white cow, that held up your train?"

Josie thought about it for a second, and then she said, "Black and white."

"I knew it!" said Miss Garble. "Holstein!"

CHAPTER
49

I WAS SO HUNGRY THAT I ordered a triple-sized, chocolate-and-vanilla swirled cone at Sparky's.

Ace had a triple too, and Penny and Josie had singles. Uncle Spiro even let us cut the line, which was already snaking down the sidewalk when we got there.

"Swell turnout!" I told him. "Congrats!"

"Thanks, squirt," said Spiro, from behind the counter. "It's a pretty grand grand opening, ain't it?"

I slurped my cone. "Maybe you should buy a permanent billboard at Orchard Field, instead of that crazy banner you rigged up in center field."

Spiro grinned so hard, his white cap almost fell off. "Pretty nifty, huh? Of course, I had to make a quick getaway during the seventh inning." He winked. "Had to be here before the game ended, so I'd be ready for the customers. Did I miss anything in the late innings?"

I wanted to tell him all about the high pop foul in the bottom of the ninth, but there was a long line of people behind me waiting for custard, so I just said, "I'll tell ya later."

I pushed my way to a corner table where Ace and Penny and Josie were sitting. Then I heard a familiar voice behind me.

"Spiro?"

I turned to look. And you wouldn't believe who I saw.

"What are you doing here, George?" said Spiro, his grin fading. "A responsible businessman like you? Shouldn't you be at the shop?"

Pop lifted his chin. "I decide to close the shop early."

"Let me guess," said Spiro. "No customers today?"

Pop didn't answer. He just surveyed the custard stand with a sour look on his face. "So this is what you do with your time? Serving ice cream for somebody named Sparky?"

"It's frozen custard," Spiro said. He leaned over the countertop. "And you may not believe this, George, but *I'm* Sparky."

Pop stood there, blinking at him. He looked around the shiny new store, and at all the happy customers slurping their custard. "Grand opening today," he said to Spiro.

"Yep."

"Sparky's?"

"Yep."

Then Pop filled his lungs and smacked the counter with an open palm. "Why Sparky's? Why not Spiro's? You worked hard to open your own ice cream store! You should be proud!"

Spiro's grin was back. "It's frozen custard, George. Chocolate or vanilla?"

Apparently Pop couldn't think of anything else to say, so he just said, "Vanilla."

And then, as he turned away from the counter with his cone, his eyes landed on me.

I gulped.

"Here comes trouble," said Ace. "Good luck, slugger." And he hustled Penny and Josie to a different corner, leaving me to deal with Pop.

"Sit down," Pop said to me, pulling out a chair from the little round table. "We must have a talk."

Uh-oh. Here it came. Might as well get it over with. I sat down to face the music.

Just then, guess who came busting through the door, all red-faced and breathing hard?

Pete.

"You!" he hollered, pointing at me across the room. "Nick cheated, Mr. Spirakis. He forged your signature. That's the only way he won the batboy contest!"

The whole crowd of people stopped slurping custard and stared.

Pete stood there, looking triumphant.

Pop stared at Pete too, and then he lifted an eyebrow and looked at me. He handed me his half-finished cone, and carefully cleaned his hands with a napkin. "You are wrong, Taki," he said, calmly but loud enough for everyone to hear. "Nicky won the contest because he was the only one who knew the answer to Mister Joe Daggett's question."

Pete's mouth dropped open, and the color drained from his face. Apparently, this was not going the way he'd expected.

Pop kept going. "You know why Nicky knew the correct answer, Taki? Because he works hard. He studies hard in school. He learns things, and he remembers things, and so when the time comes to use the knowledge, he is ready. That is why my Nicky won the batboy contest."

And he turned his back on Pete, plucked the half-eaten cone from my hand, and took a bite.

My pop. He's the best.

"But—but—he cheated!" sputtered Pete.

I stood up with a scrape of my chair, and sidled my way through the crowd to where Pete was standing. "You got a lot of nerve," I told him. "Maybe I should tell *your* ma where I got the idea of forging a parent's signature."

Pete's eyes got big, and his face went red. (Because he

is one of the many people in the world with a healthy fear of the Queen of England.) He clenched his hands into fists, and he opened his mouth to say something, but then he closed it again and stomped out the door.

And that's the first time I ever saw a twelve-year-old kid walk out of a frozen custard stand without any custard.

Everybody went back to eating custard and having fun. Except me and Pop.

"What Taki said is true?" said Pop, when I sat down again at the little table. It wasn't really a question.

I nodded.

"Because I would not sign the form for Mister Daggett's contest." He sighed and shook his head. "I am disappointed in you, Nicky. Sneaking around, just to go to a baseball game?"

We looked at each other, and I could tell he realized how lame that sounded, after I'd caught him doing the same thing, more or less.

Pop gave me a guilty grin. He munched his cone thoughtfully. Finally, he laid a hand on my shoulder. "I tell you many times, Nicky, that hard work is very important. And I saw you working hard today, on that baseball field. Even though you lied, you make me proud today." He took another bite of his cone. "I haven't been to a ball game in a long time. It was lots of fun. I forgot that having fun sometimes is important too. Hard work *and* fun— that's American, *neh*? I think from now on you should work only half days on Saturday. Finished at noon. *Neh*?"

I almost couldn't believe my ears. "Really? That'd be swell, Pop. Thanks."

"But first you are grounded for two weeks. Except for Greek school."

Sometimes you have to take what you can get.

Then he leaned close to me. "Listen, Nicky, don't tell your mama I went to the ball game. She likes the baseball too, but I remembered that she had a very important meeting at the church, so I went by myself." Then he started chuckling to himself. "Those monkeys . . ." He laughed and slapped his knee.

"Gee, Pop . . . ," I started. But I wasn't sure if I should say anything. All I could think about was how everyone in my family *thought* they were good at keeping secrets, when they were actually *terrible* at keeping secrets.

"George!"

Me and Pop both jumped and turned around.

Pop jumped again. "Athena? What are you doing here?"

"What are *you* doing here?" said Ma, the flowers on her hat jiggling in indignation. "Why are you not at the shop?"

"Why are *you* not at the church?"

Ma's look of indignation melted into a sort of guilty shrug. "The meeting, it was very short." She adjusted her hat and coughed.

"Oh, well," said Pop, accepting the challenge of good

excuses, "the shop, it was very quiet today. No customers. I closed up early."

Ma nodded slowly, and then she actually gave Pop the stink-eye. "How you found out about this new ice cream shop?"

"Frozen custard," said Pop. "Uhh . . ."

And then I knew the jig was up. Because the only way either Ma or Pop could've known about Sparky's was if they'd seen the banner in center field. At the ballpark.

But Pop wasn't ready to admit defeat. He smiled in relief and put a hand on my shoulder. "Nicky told me!"

"Gee whiz, Pop!" Can you believe the nerve? It's one thing to lie to your parents. But to see your parents lying to each other, and using *you* as an excuse? What was the world coming to?

"Wait a minute . . . ," said Pop, and now *he* was giving *Ma* the stink-eye. "What do I see there in your pocketbook?"

Ma frowned and looked down at her purse. There was a small piece of paper sticking out.

Pop pointed and sputtered, "That—that is a ticket stub. You went to the ball game!"

Ma gasped, but then she said the only thing she could say. "It was Ladies' Day. Half price."

And then Pop busted out laughing. He fished in his pocket, and showed her *his* ticket stub, and Ma busted out laughing too.

CHAPTER

50

$\mathcal{I}$ NEVER KNEW MA COULD pack it away like that. She ordered a triple cone and ate the whole thing. I guess standing up to the Queen of England gave her an appetite. I introduced Ma and Pop to Penny and Josie, and they didn't even say anything about Josie's short skirt, even though I knew they were thinking it.

That's when the bell jingled on the shop door. A man stood in the doorway, wearing an overcoat and hat.

"Well, well, well," said Joe Daggett, limping into the shop and looking around. "So this is the notorious Sparky's."

For the second time in a few minutes, the whole crowd fell silent. From behind the counter, Spiro gulped.

Joe Daggett sidled up to the counter and eyed Spiro. "Are you Sparky?"

Spiro's face was a blend of guilt and pride. "That's me," he admitted. "Spiro, actually. Spiro Spirakis. Nice to meet you?" He warily offered a hand.

Joe Daggett busted out in a huge smile. "Spirakis? Are you George's little brother?" He laughed. "I should've known that get-up-and-go runs in the family. I wanted to shake the hand of the genius who unfurled that banner out in center field. If this ice cream business of yours ever goes bust, I could use you in the Mudpuppies front office, running promotions!"

Spiro grinned and pumped Joe Daggett's hand. "Gee, thanks, Mr. Daggett," he said. "And by the way, it's frozen custard."

Uncle Spiro had just served up a double chocolate cone to Joe Daggett when in walked *real* trouble.

"Hello there, Spiro!" sang ol' Sophie Costas. "I heard you opened a custard stand, and so of course I had to see it for myself!" She smiled with her red painted lips.

"Oh," said Spiro, barely looking up. "Hiya, Sophie. Chocolate or vanilla?"

"Oh, golly, no thanks!" said Sophie, smoothing her dress. "I'm watching my figure." She batted her eyelashes.

And that's exactly the time Josie happened to say, from the table in the corner, "That was the best custard I've ever had. I think I'll have another one." She got up and moseyed her way to the counter, not even noticing Sophie giving her the evil eye.

Behind the counter, Uncle Spiro straightened his bow tie. "We haven't met," he said to Josie, in her Kenosha Comets uniform with the skirt that was too short. But he didn't look at her legs at all. He just looked her in the eye. "I'm Sparky—I mean, Spiro. How d'ya do?"

"How d'ya do?" Josie said back.

"So you're the AWOL girl baseball player," he said.

Josie laughed and nodded. "My train was held hostage by a cow."

"Well, if that don't beat all," said Spiro. "Jersey or Holstein? Or maybe it was a Brown Swiss. Did you know that the best frozen custard is made with milk from Brown Swiss cows?"

"You don't say," said Josie. "That's very interesting."

And that's when Sophie left in a huff. For some reason.

● ● ●

Uncle Spiro's grand opening was a big hit. He had to close the doors early when he completely ran out of custard. So we all helped him clean up, and Pop even offered to shine his shoes for free any time he needed it, because "a businessman, he needs the spiffy shoes."

"But why you can't call it Spiro's Custard?" Pop asked. "You are not proud of your name? Your heritage?"

"Sure I am, George. But you tell me: Why isn't it Spirakis's Shoe Repair and Hat Shop?"

Pop thought about that for a minute. And then his face relaxed into his usual smile, and he said, "Sparky's Custard. I like it. It's American, *neh*?"

Then Pop reached out and shook Spiro's hand. Which goes to show, there's a first time for everything.

"But don't ever forget where you come from," said Pop.

Spiro laughed. "Don't worry, George. I couldn't forget if I tried."

That got him a big fat pinch on the cheek.

And that's when me and Ace and Penny got the heck out of there.

"Say, Penny," I said as we walked to the streetcar stop in the fading daylight. "You wanna join our Scramble team?"

"Scramble? What's that?"

"You know," said Ace. "Baseball, in the zoo. It's fun."

"I don't know . . . ," she said. "What about Pete?"

That was a good question.

"You know what I think?" I said. "I think Pete needs a personal introduction to Tank."

"Yeah," said Ace. "Let's see how *he* likes it in right field. Too bad no one ever hits the ball to right field."

That's when I looked over at Penny, and she looked back at me.

"Except left-handed hitters," I said. "Gee. I wonder where we could find a left-handed hitter?"

Ace stopped dead in his tracks. "Penny! *You're* a lefty!"

She grinned. "Yep."

"I bet you could hit the ball over the right-field fence," said Ace.

"I bet I could," she said, with her usual modesty.

"And I bet we could arrange for you to come to bat when Pete is playing right field," I said.

"I suppose so," said Penny. "And then what?"

"Then," said Ace, giving her a thumbs-up, "Tank will take care of the rest."

Penny gasped. "You wouldn't let anyone really get hurt, would you? I mean, I know it's Pete, but still—"

"Don't worry, I know how to handle Tank," I told her. I held up my crossed fingers. "Me and Tank, we're like *this*."

"What do ya say, Penny?" said Ace. "We need you on the team."

"I'll think about it," she said. A few blocks away, the lights at Orchard Field switched off, one by one. "The zoo sure is a crazy place to play ball."

But I knew better. "It's the best place in the whole wide world."

ACKNOWLEDGMENTS

I owe a huge debt of gratitude to:

Tim Wild, Trish Khan, and especially Mary Kazmierczak, of the Milwaukee County Zoo, who answered questions, shared their passion, and gave me access to the zoo's collection of photos and archives.

My writer buddies, for their advice and encouragement: Dori Chaconas, Kim Marcus, Audrey Vernick, and the Wednesday Writers Who Meet on Tuesdays.

My editor, Karen Wojtyla, for her votes of confidence, her unerring instinct, and for the extra at-bats in the late innings.

My agent, Tracey Adams, for always, always, always being there.

Spiro Chaconas and Dio Deley, for help with Greek vocabulary.

And to Nick Chaconas, who shared his childhood stories, and who let me reweave them into a new tapestry.

AUTHOR'S NOTE

The Washington Park Zoo in Milwaukee, Wisconsin, occupied one corner of a large city park and served as a playground for neighborhood kids. Close encounters with animals were common (though not always reported to adults). Exactly as Nick describes in the story, "a stone wall topped with a chest-high chain-link fence" was the only thing that separated humans from large horned beasts.

Milwaukee's zoo has long since moved, but Washington Park is still there, and so is that fence.

The zoo's annual Spring Opening was a big deal. The day featured brass bands, speeches, and the much-anticipated release of the monkeys from their winter quarters onto Monkey Island. The island featured a water-filled moat that the monkeys swam in but could not climb out of to escape their enclosure. They really could get almost close enough to touch.

A "Great Circus Parade" was a tradition in Milwaukee for many years. Colorful wagons carried giraffes, lions, and other exotic animals through the downtown streets to celebrate the annual arrival of the circus. In an echo of that tradition, the Washington Park Zoo sponsored its own traveling zoo wagon, which trundled around the city each summer so kids could get a closer look at a few of the animals.

A rhinoceros never escaped from its wagon, but once it almost did. In 1943, a rhino was purchased from the Brookfield Zoo in Chicago, coaxed into a wooden crate, and trucked the ninety miles to Milwaukee, accompanied by a police escort and a zookeeper with an elephant gun. According to the official report, "Whenever the procession halted, [the rhino] became rampageous. . . . At each stop, he hit the front end of his crate a succession of terrific wallops, his horned nose catapulted by his 2,500 pounds. . . . So terrific were his onslaughts that everyone in the parade feared he would gain freedom."

Joe Daggett's character was inspired by Bill Veeck, prominent in baseball for over forty years and owner of the minor league Milwaukee Brewers from 1941 to 1945. Veeck (who had a wooden leg as a result of wounds received during World War II) was a fervent believer in having fun at the ballpark. His groundbreaking ideas have become synonymous with baseball: fireworks-shooting scoreboards, fan giveaways, names on players' uniforms, and even the ivy in Chicago's Wrigley Field.

Veeck once sponsored a batboy contest, inviting boys to write an essay explaining why they wanted the job. Thousands of essays were submitted, including one entry from a girl. She received a polite letter from Mr. Veeck, explaining that only boys were eligible to win.

Orchard Field, the old wooden ballpark "at Eighth and Chalmers," is modeled after Borchert Field (at Eighth and Chambers streets) in Milwaukee. "The Orchard" was home to minor league and barnstorming baseball for many years, hosting players such as Lou Gehrig, Babe Ruth, and Satchel Paige. It was torn down in 1953.

The All-American Girls Professional Baseball League (AAGPBL) had ten teams in 1948, including the Kenosha Comets. The players pitched overhand, and their uniforms included short skirts.

Nick was a real twelve-year-old who lived two blocks from the zoo. He really did hop that short fence to get his baseball out of the animal yard. His parents were immigrants from Greece and had an arranged marriage. Nick shined shoes in his father's hat shop. His mother picked dandelion greens to cook for supper.

Nick is my dad.

For more background information, photos,
and reading lists, please visit my website at
STACYDEKEYSER.COM.

Turn the page
for a sneak peek at
The Brixen Witch.

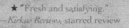

THE
BRIXEN
WITCH

★ "Fresh and satisfying."
—*Kirkus Reviews*, starred review

STACY DEKEYSER

RUDI BAUER ran for his life and cursed his bad luck. He would never have touched the gold coin — much less put it in his pocket — if he'd known it belonged to a witch.

It had been a blustery morning, with more than a hint of snow stinging his nostrils, when Rudi left his warm cottage and climbed the high meadow to hunt rabbits in the shadow of the Berg. All day long he scrambled on the mountain, but his aim was crooked, or perhaps it was his slingshot. By dusk, icy pellets stabbed Rudi's hands and face, and he had nothing to show for the day but the golden guilder in his pocket and its rightful owner flinging hexes down the mountain in his wake.

So now here he was, half running, half stumbling downslope, the wind and sleet screaming in his ears.

Or was it the witch?

Rudi didn't stop to find out. He hurtled down the mountain, his legs threatening to give way and send him off the edge and onto the rocks below.

But he wasn't thinking of that. Or he was trying not to. He was thinking how remarkable it was that the witch was real after all. All this time, he'd assumed she was nothing but a fairy tale; a bedtime fable told to every child in the village of Brixen. His own mother had often told him the story of the Brixen Witch, who lived under the mountain, hidden and silent so long as no one disturbed her domain.

He had never liked that story at bedtime. It did not result in happy dreams.

And other than a few stories, nothing much was said about the witch in Brixen. People said it was bad luck to talk of such things.

"So I found the entrance to her lair," thought Rudi to himself as darkness fell and the lights of the village appeared below through the slanting pellets of ice. "I wonder if anyone else knows where it is. I wonder if I'd ever be able to find it again."

But he couldn't imagine ever wanting to find it again. Every blink of his eyes brought a flash of memory: the gaping mouth; the teeth like spikes; the foul icy breath. And the screech—it had been painful to his ears, like a thousand cats fighting in a room with walls of stone.

Rudi shuddered as he hurled himself toward his own front door. One last look over his shoulder. One last ear-piercing shriek that may have been the storm, but may have been—

And he crashed into the house, somersaulting onto the floor as the door hit the wall with a bang. In one quick instant he was surrounded by everyone he loved most dearly in the world, and he had never been happier to see them.

"Close the door, boy!" yelled his father, jumping from his chair and spilling his pipe onto Rudi's head. "You're letting October into the house!"

"By the saints!" said his mother. "You're muddy as a salamander. And now look at my rug."

"Where are the rabbits?" said Oma. "I'm getting too old to eat my dinner so late."

Rudi blinked up at them, trying to catch his breath. He swallowed hard, lifted his head, and croaked, "Witch." Then he collapsed into a heap.

"Which what?" said Oma, *tsk*ing and nudging Rudi with her toe. "The boy needs to learn to speak up. I don't see any rabbits on his belt."

"Nor do I," said his mother, sighing. "Then it's barley soup again."

Rudi sat up, dug pipe ash out of his ear, and tried to speak calmly. But all he could manage was, "A cave . . . on the mountain . . . something chased me. . . ."

"What was it?" said his father. "A bear? A wolf?" He squinted at Rudi. "A bad-tempered marmot?"

"Should have shot it anyway," said Oma. "It would have been as tasty as rabbit, I'm sure." She smacked her gums.

Rudi regarded his slingshot and his grandmother in turn. "It was bigger than me," he told her. "With teeth. And claws. And a screech like the Devil himself."

"Rudolf Augustin Bauer!" scolded his mother. "Such stories you tell!"

Rudi considered that the stories he told were only those she'd told him first, but he kept silent in that regard.

Rudi's father refilled the bowl of his pipe and struck a match. "Your eyes were playing tricks on you, son. You know better than to be caught up there as the light wanes, especially when a storm threatens. Are you sure you didn't come upon a fox sleeping in its den? That would raise a snarl, I've no doubt." And he snorted and clapped Rudi on the back, so that Rudi nearly collapsed again onto the rug.

Rudi sighed. His father must be right. It had been getting dark, and the snow had started to fly, and it had become difficult to see. He smiled crookedly, and felt his face grow warm, and scratched the back of his head.

"You're right, Papa," he said. "That was it. I'm sure it was a fox." And Rudi stood on the rug, kicked off his muddy boots (to his mother's exasperation), and took himself up the stairs to clean up.

But as he pulled off his grass-stained trousers, a new thought popped into his head. He plunged his hand deep into his pocket, and his fingers closed around something hard and flat and round.

A golden guilder.

It gleamed softly, even in the dimness of the loft, and it was unlike anything he'd ever seen. Not that he'd often seen any gold coin up close before. But it had a thickness about it, and markings he couldn't read.

"What kind of fox keeps an old gold coin in its den?" he whispered to himself. But he decided it was just coincidence. If Rudi had stumbled upon the cave, why not someone else? Another hunter had dropped the coin long ago, and today Rudi had found it. That was all.

His mind wandered to what he might be able to buy with such a coin. A new pair of skis? A new rug for his mother? A slingshot that actually worked?

And then one ragged syllable burst from Oma's mouth, flew up the stairs, and scraped Rudi's eardrums.

"Witch!"

Rudi's breath stopped in his throat. The coin fell from his hand onto his stockinged foot and rolled under his bed. He stifled a curse.

"Which what?" boomed Papa's voice from below. Then he laughed. "Is that how you play the game, Mother?"

Rudi scrambled into clean trousers, fumbled beneath the bed for the coin, and jammed it under his pillow. "How's that, Oma?" he called over the railing, his voice cracking.

"When you first spilled into the house all breathless and red in the face," she called up to him, "you said 'witch.' Didn't you?" Oma's mind was sharp. It was her ears that sometimes lagged behind, but they always caught up eventually, and that's what they were doing now.

Rudi gulped, and resisted the urge to glance back at his pillow. "I was being silly," he called down. "Like Papa said—it was a trick of the light."

Oma squinted up at him for a moment. Then she shrugged and sat herself down to dinner. "As you say. You were there, not I."

Rudi breathed a sigh of relief, which brought the aroma of hot barley soup and fried apples to his nostrils. He bounded down the stairs, his appetite surging.

"All I mean to say," said Oma, as if the conversation had not just ended, "is that if you did visit a witch, I hope you didn't take anything. Anyone who steals from the Brixen Witch's hoard is hounded without mercy until she gets her treasure back. That's all I mean to say."

And Oma dipped her spoon into her bowl and slurped her soup.

Looking for another great book?
Find it
IN THE MIDDLE.

Fun, fantastic books for kids
in the in-be**TWEEN** age.

IntheMiddleBooks.com

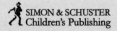 SIMON & SCHUSTER
Children's Publishing   f /SimonKids   @SimonKids

EXPERIENCE THE MAGIC AND MISCHIEF
OF THE BOGGART AND HIS FRIENDS
IN THIS CLASSIC SERIES FROM
NEWBERY MEDAL WINNER SUSAN COOPER

"As long as writers with Susan Cooper's skill
continue to publish, magic is always available."
—*New York Times Book Review*

★"A lively story, compelling from first page to last."
—*School Library Journal*, starred review of *The Boggart*

★"An imaginative and compelling tale."
—*Publishers Weekly*, starred review of *The Boggart and the Monster*

"The Boggart remains as comical, fey, unpredictable,
and thoroughly entertaining as ever."
—*Kirkus Reviews*, on *The Boggart Fights Back*

PRINT AND EBOOK EDITIONS AVAILABLE
From Margaret K. McElderry Books
simonandschuster.com/kids

Buck discovers that his favorite book series might be less fictional than he thought.

HOLY TROLLS! WHAT'S A SUPERFAN TO DO?

GNOME-A-GEDDON

★"Buck survives to show emotional resilience . . . and Holt leaves him, along with readers, eager for a sequel."
–***BOOKLIST*, STARRED REVIEW**

"Fans of Angie Sage's Magyk, J. R. R. Tolkien's *The Lord of the Rings*, and C.S. Lewis's *The Chronicles of Narnia* should enjoy this."
–**SLJ**

"This is silly, clever fun for fantasy buffs."
–***BCCB***

From **MARGARET K. McELDERRY BOOKS**
simonandschuster.com/kids

PRINT AND EBOOK EDITIONS AVAILABLE